"Dream on, Alpha Man."

His eyes crinkled mischievously at the corners. "Alpha Man?"

Had she really *said* that? She must be punchier than she thought.

"It was an insult. A friendly one." Hope bit down on an oath. She was just making it worse.

He laughed, his husky baritone like music to her ears. Continued giving her the long, sexy once-over. "Sounded more like a compliment to me."

He was twisting everything around, embarrassing her and putting her off her game. Indignant, she trod closer. "Of course you would think that."

He held his ground, arms folded in front of him. Again, that long, steady appraisal. "Because I'm alpha?"

He definitely was not a beta man.

"Can we end this repartee?"

He gathered her in his arms. "With pleasure."

"What are you doing?"

"What any *alpha* male would do in this situation." Grinning, he lowe

D1100766

3169035

A TEXAS SOLDIER'S FAMILY

BY
CATHY GILLEN THACKER

MILLS & BOON

All rights reserved including the right of reproduction in whole or in part in any form. This edition is published by arrangement with Harlequin Books S.A.

This is a work of fiction. Names, characters, places, locations and incidents are purely fictional and bear no relationship to any real life individuals, living or dead, or to any actual places, business establishments, locations, events or incidents. Any resemblance is entirely coincidental.

This book is sold subject to the condition that it shall not, by way of trade or otherwise, be lent, resold, hired out or otherwise circulated without the prior consent of the publisher in any form of binding or cover other than that in which it is published and without a similar condition including this condition being imposed on the subsequent purchaser.

® and ™ are trademarks owned and used by the trademark owner and/or its licensee. Trademarks marked with ® are registered with the United Kingdom Patent Office and/or the Office for Harmonisation in the Internal Market and in other countries.

First Published in Great Britain 2016
By Mills & Boon, an imprint of HarperCollins*Publishers*
1 London Bridge Street, London, SE1 9GF

© 2016 Cathy Gillen Thacker

ISBN: 978-0-263-92005-5

23-0716

Our policy is to use papers that are natural, renewable and recyclable products and made from wood grown in sustainable forests. The logging and manufacturing processes conform to the legal environmental regulations of the country of origin.

Printed and bound in Spain
by CPI, Barcelona

Cathy Gillen Thacker is married and a mother of three. She and her husband spent eighteen years in Texas and now reside in North Carolina. Her mysteries, romantic comedies and heartwarming family stories have made numerous appearances on bestseller lists, but her best reward, she says, is knowing one of her books made someone's day a little brighter. A popular Mills & Boon author for many years, she loves telling passionate stories with happy endings and thinks nothing beats a good romance and a hot cup of tea! You can visit Cathy's website, www.cathygillenthacker.com, for more information on her upcoming and previously published books, recipes and a list of her favorite things.

ABERDEENSHIRE LIBRARIES	
3189035	
Bertrams	23/06/2016
ROM Pbk	£3.99

Chapter One

"Welcome aboard!" The flight attendant smiled. "Going home to Texas…?"

"Not voluntarily," Garrett Lockhart muttered under his breath as he made his way through the aircraft to his seat in the fourth row.

It wasn't that he didn't *appreciate* spending time with his family, he acknowledged, stowing his bag in the bulkhead and stuffing his six-foot-five-inch body into the first-class seat next to the window. He did.

It's just that he didn't want them weighing in on what his next step should be. Or what he should do with his inheritance. The decision was hard enough. Should he sell out or stay and build a life in Laramie, as his late father had wanted?

Reenlist and take the considerable promotion being offered?

Or take a civilian post that would allow him to pursue his dreams?

He had twenty-nine days to decide.

And an unspecified but pressing family crisis to handle in the meantime.

And an expensive-looking blonde in a white power suit who'd been sizing him up from a distance, ever since he arrived at the gate…

He'd noticed her, too. Hard not to with that delicately gorgeous face, a mane of long, silky hair brushing against her shoulders, and a smoking-hot body that just wouldn't quit.

Two years ago…before Leanne…he might have taken her up on her invitation…

But his failed engagement had taught him too well. He wasn't interested in any woman hell-bent on climbing her way to the top.

He wanted a partner who understood what was important in life. Not a woman who couldn't stop doing business even long enough to board a plane. She'd been talking on her cell phone nonstop and was still on it as she stepped into the cabin. With a thousand-watt smile aimed his way, oblivious to the three backpack-clad college boys queued up like dominoes behind her, she continued on down the aisle, checking her ticket for her seat assignment as she walked.

Phone to her ear, one hand trying to retract the telescoping handle of her suitcase while still managing the equally roomy carryall over her shoulder, she said, "…have to go… yes, yes. I'll call you as soon as I land in Dallas. Not to worry." She laughed softly, charmingly, while shooting him another glance and lifting her suitcase with one hand into the overhead compartment. "I always do…"

Annoyed, he turned his attention to the tarmac and was watching bags being loaded into the cargo hold when, in the aisle behind him, commotion suddenly erupted.

"If you-all will just *wait* until I can—*ouch!*" He heard the pretty blonde stumble toward him, yelping as her expensive leather carryall tumbled off her shoulder and crashed onto his lap. Her elbow landed hard against his skull, just above his ear, while a pair of sumptuous breasts burrowed into his face. Only the quick defensive movement of his right arm kept the lady exec's head from smashing into the wall above the airplane window.

However, nothing could be done to stop the off-kilter weight of her from sprawling inelegantly across his thighs, while the trio of impatient college kids responsible for her abrupt exit from the aisle continued unapologetically toward the rear of the plane.

She lifted her head, regarding him with a stunned expression as their eyes met. Heat swept her pretty face. He inhaled a whiff of vanilla and—lavender, maybe? All he knew for sure, he thought, as he heard her moan softly in dismay and felt his own body harden in response, was that everything about this woman was incredibly sexy.

Too sexy…

Too tall…

Too everything…

"Ma'am?" he rasped, trying not to think what it would be like to have this sweet-smelling bundle of femininity beneath him in bed. Never mind just how long it had been…

With effort, he called on every ounce of military reserve he had, sucked in a breath and looked straight into her wide, emerald-green eyes. "Are you all right?"

THIS, HOPE WINSLOW thought with an embarrassed grimace, was not how her day was supposed to go. Seven months out of the workplace might have left her a *little* rusty. But completely without social skills or enough balance to stay on her feet no matter how hard she'd been shoved?

Furthermore, it wasn't as if she had *wanted* to take that last call from the client. She'd had no choice. She needed the income and acclaim this job was going to bring in, and like it or not, high-paying clients required high-level hand-holding. Plus, she had a soft spot in her heart for this current one…and that made any of Lucille's requests difficult to resist.

But her quarry—the guy she had accidentally fallen on—would likely not understand any of that.

Resolved to retain whatever small amount of dignity she had left, Hope forced another small—apologetic—smile, inhaled deeply, then put her left hand down on the armrest beneath the window and shoved herself upright. Only it wasn't an armrest, she swiftly found out. There wasn't one there. It was the rock-hard denim-clad upper thigh of the man who'd caught her in his arms.

Mortified, she plucked her fingers away before they encountered anything else untoward. Then she promptly lost her balance, fell again and had the point of her elbow land where her hand had been.

Her gallant seatmate let out an *oomph* and looked alarmed. With good reason, Hope thought.

Another inch to the left and…!

"Let me help you," he drawled, his voice a smooth Texas-accented rumble. With one hand hooked around her waist and the other around her shoulders, he lifted her quickly and skillfully to her feet, then turned and lowered her so her bottom landed squarely in her own seat. That done, he handed her the leather carryall she'd inadvertently assaulted him with.

Hope knew she should say something. If only to make her later job easier.

And she would have, if the sea-blue eyes she'd been staring into hadn't been so mesmerizing. She liked his hair, too. So dark and thick and…touchable…

The pictures she had seen of him and his siblings hadn't done him justice. Or indicated just how big and broad shouldered he was. Enough to make her own five-eleven frame feel dainty…

And heaven knew *that* didn't happen every day. Even in Texas.

"Ma'am?" he prodded again, less patiently.

Clearly he was expecting some response to ease the unabashed sexual tension that had sprung up between them, so she tore her eyes from the way his black knit polo shirt molded the sinewy contours of his chest and taut abs, and said the first thing that came into her mind. "Thank you for your assistance just now. And for your service. To our country, I mean."

His dark brow furrowed. His lips—so firm and sensual—thinned. Shoulders flexing, he studied her with breathtaking intent, then asked, "How'd you know I was in the military?"

IT WAS A simple question, Garrett thought.

One that shouldn't have required any dissembling.

But dissembling was precisely what his seatmate appeared to be doing as she discreetly tugged the skirt of her elegant, white business suit lower on her shapely thighs, then leaned forward to place her bag beneath the seat in front of her, as per preflight requirements.

"Um…your hair," she said finally.

Oh, yeah. Military cut. Made sense.

"Well, that and the duffel in the overhead." She glanced at the passengers seated across the aisle, a young mother and a child with a *Dora the Explorer* backpack. The rest of the luggage stored above them was pink. Whereas his, he knew, was army green.

Point made, she sat back and drew the safety restraint across her lap, once again drawing his attention where it definitely should not be. "So, how long have you been in the military?" she asked pleasantly.

He watched as she fit the metal buckle into the clasp, drew it taut. Was there any part of her not delectable? he wondered. Any inch of her he did not want? "Eight years." And why was it suddenly so hard to get the words out?

She wet her lips. Suddenly sounding a little hoarse, too, she inquired, "And what do you do?"

"I'm a physician."

She pursed her lips in a way that had him wondering what it would be like to kiss her. "Which must make you a…?"

Not just kiss her. Make love to her. Hot, wild, passionate love, he thought, drinking in the soft, womanly scent of her. "Captain," he said.

She extended a hand. It was as velvety soft as it looked, her grip warm and firm. "Well, it's nice to meet you, Captain…?"

He let her go reluctantly, the awareness he'd felt when she'd landed in his lap returning, full force. "Lockhart. Garrett Lockhart."

Her expression turned even more welcoming. She studied him intently. "I'm Hope Winslow."

Okay, so maybe his first impression of her hadn't been on point. Even if she wasn't his type, there were worse ways to pass the time than sitting next to a charming, gorgeous woman. And she *was* gorgeous, Garrett reflected, feeling a little unsettled and a lot attracted as the plane backed away from the gate and the flight attendants went through the safety instructions.

Tall enough to fit nicely against him. With legs that were made for high heels and curves that just wouldn't quit pushing against the taut fabric of her sleek summer suit. Honey-blond hair as straight and silky as spun gold brushed her shoulders and long bangs fell to frame her oval face. Her features were elegant, her bow-shaped lips soft, pink and full, her emerald eyes radiating wit and keen intelligence.

He doubted there was anything she set her mind to that she didn't get. Her ringless left hand said she was single.

It was too bad he wasn't in the market for a high-maintenance, high-powered career woman.

"So what do you do for a living?" he asked, after the flight attendant had come by to deliver bowls of warmed nuts and take their drink orders. Milk for her, coffee for him.

She picked out an almond. Then a pecan. "I'm in scandal management."

Okay, he could see that.

She seemed like the type who could take a highly emotional, probably volatile situation and boil it down to something manageable. "I recently started my own firm." She reached into a pocket of her carryall and plucked out a business card. *Winslow Strategies. Crisis Management by the Very Best.* It had her name featured prominently, printed in the same memorable green as her eyes, and a Dallas address.

He started to hand it back. She gestured for him to keep it, so he slipped it into the pocket of his shirt. "Business good?"

She gestured affably, looking reluctant to be too specific. "There's always someone in trouble."

I'll bet. "But to have to hire someone to get yourself out of it?" He couldn't keep the contempt from his voice.

"People hire lawyers all the time when they find themselves in a tight spot."

Imagining that line worked on a lot of very wealthy people, he sipped his coffee. "Not the same thing."

She turned slightly toward him, tilting her head. "It sort of is," she said, her voice a little too tight. "Words can hurt. Or mislead. Or falsely indict. So can actions." She paused to sip her milk and let her words sink in, then set her glass down on the tray. "It's important when in the midst of a potentially life-altering, and especially life-damaging event, to have someone on your side who isn't emotionally involved, calling the shots and orchestrating everything behind the scenes."

Her exceptional calmness rankled; he couldn't say why. "Creating a publicly acceptable narrative," he reiterated.

She lifted a delicate hand, gesturing amiably. "I prefer to think of it as a compelling explanation that will allow others to empathize with you. And, if not exactly approve of or condone, at least understand."

"And therefore let your client off the hook," he said grimly, reflecting on another time. Another situation. And another woman whose actions he resented to this day. "Whether they deserve to be spared any accountability for what they've done or not."

Taken aback, Hope Winslow squinted at him. "Are you speaking personally?"

Hell, yes, it had been personal! Being cheated on and then backed into a corner always was. Not that he regretted protecting the innocent bystanders in the situation. They'd done nothing to deserve having their names dragged through the mud.

"I'm guessing that's a yes," she said.

The silence stretched between them, awkward now. She continued to look him up and down, asking finally, "Are you always this black and white in your thinking, Captain Lockhart?"

His turn to shrug. He finished what was left of his coffee. "About some things, yeah." He set the cup down with a thud. The flight attendant appeared with a refill.

When they were alone again, Hope continued curiously, "Is that why you chose the military as a career?"

It was part of it. The rest was more personal. "Both my

grandfathers served our country." His dad had passed on the opportunity. He and one of his four siblings had not.

"And…?" she prodded.

He exhaled, not above admitting that honor was everything to him. "There's not a lot of room for error—or gray areas—in the military. It's either right or it's wrong." *Simple. Basic. Necessary.* Unlike the way he'd grown up.

She stared at him. "And you think what I do is wrong."

"I wouldn't have put it that way," Garrett said.

A delicate pale brow arched. "But you think it, don't you?"

Wishing she hadn't put him on the spot, he returned her sharp, assessing gaze. "You're right. I do."

"Well, that's too bad, Captain." Hope Winslow took a deep breath that lifted her opulent breasts. "Because your mother, Lucille Lockhart, has hired me to represent your entire family, as well as the Lockhart Foundation."

He took a moment to let the blonde's announcement sink in. Feeling as if he had just taken a sucker punch to the gut, he grumbled, "So the way you kept checking me out before we boarded, the fact that we're both seated in first class on this flight, side by side, was no accident."

"Lucille said you'd be difficult. I needed to talk with you before we landed and I wanted to get started early. And to that end…"

She finished her milk, put her tray away, retrieved her carryall from beneath the seat and took out a computer tablet. She brought up a screen titled Talking Points for Lockhart Foundation Crisis and set it in front of him. "I want you to memorize these."

One hand on the cup, lest it spill, he stared at her. "You have got to be kidding me."

The hell of it was, she wasn't. "There's a press conference later today," she informed him crisply, suddenly all business. "We need you to be ready."

This was like a replay of his past, only in a more formal venue. He hadn't played those games then, and he certainly wasn't getting sucked into them now. "No."

Hope leaned closer, her green eyes narrowing. "You have to be there." Her tone said the request was nonnegotiable.

His mood had been grim when he got on the plane. It was fire and brimstone now. No wonder his mother hadn't wanted to be specific when she'd sent out that vague but somewhat hysterical SOS and let him know he was needed in Dallas ASAP.

He worked his jaw back and forth. "Why? I don't have anything to do with the family charity."

"You're on the board of directors."

Which basically did nothing but meet a couple times a year and green light—by voice vote—everything the CEO and CFO requested. "So are my mother and all my siblings."

"All of whom have been asked to participate and follow the plan." Hope paused, even more purposefully. "Your mother needs you to stand beside her."

Garrett imagined that was so. Lucille had been vulnerable since his dad's death. Knowing how much his parents had loved each other, that they'd been together for over forty years, he imagined the loss his mom felt was even more palpable than his own.

But there were limits as to what he would do. In this situation or any other. "And I will," he promised tautly. "Just not like a puppet on a string. And certainly not in any scripted way in front of any microphones."

ONE LOOK AT the dark expression on Garrett's face told Hope there was no convincing him otherwise. Not while they were on the plane, anyway.

So she remained quiet during the descent. Thinking. Strategizing.

By the time the aircraft landed in Dallas, she knew what she had to do.

She waited for him to catch up after they'd left the Jetway and walked out into the terminal, dragging her overnight bag behind her. "Your mother is sending a limo for us."

He slung his duffel over one brawny shoulder. "Thanks. I'll find my own way home." He turned in the direction of the rental cars.

Hope rushed to catch up, her long strides no match for his. "She's expecting us at the foundation office downtown."

"Okay."

Desperate to keep Garrett Lockhart from getting away from her entirely, she caught his arm, steering him off to the side, out of the way of other travelers. "Okay, you'll be there?" she asked, as amazed at the strength and heat in the powerful biceps as by the building awareness inside of her. She had to curtail this desire. She could not risk another romantic interlude like the last. Could not!

One second she'd been holding on to him. Now he had dropped his duffel and was holding on to her. Hands curved lightly around her upper arms, oblivious to the curious stares of onlookers, he backed her up against a pillar, his tall, powerful physique caging hers. The muscles in his jaw bunched. "Get this through that pretty little head of yours. You are not in charge of me."

Like heck she wasn't! This was her job, gosh darn it. Refusing to be intimidated by this handsome bear of a man she lifted her chin. Valiantly tried again. "This crisis…"

He stared her down. "What crisis?"

He had a right to know what they were dealing with,

but best they not delve into the exact details here, with people passing by right and left. She swallowed in the face of all that raw testosterone, the feel of his hands cupping her shoulders, the wish that... Never mind what she wished! "I'd prefer..."

He didn't wait to hear the rest. Pivoting, he picked up his olive-green duffel, slung it back over his shoulder and headed for the doors out of Terminal B.

She raced after him, her trim skirt and high heels no match for his long, masterful strides. She would have lost him entirely had it not been for the contingent waiting on the other side.

No sooner had he cleared the glass doors than a group with press badges rushed toward him, trailing his sixty-eight-year-old mother.

As usual, the willowy brunette socialite was garbed in a sophisticated sheath and cardigan, her trademark pearls around her neck. Despite the many conversations they'd had this morning, Lucille Lockhart also looked more frazzled than she had the last time Hope had seen her. Not a good sign.

"Garrett, darling!" Lucille cried, rushing forward to envelope her much taller son in a fierce familial hug, the kind returning military always got from their loved ones.

Just that quickly, microphones were shoved into his face. "Captain Garrett! What do you think about the broken promises to area nonprofits?" a brash redhead demanded while cameras whirred and lightbulbs went off.

"Were you in on the decision not to pay them what was promised?" another reporter shouted.

"Does your family want the beneficiary charities to fail in their missions? Or did they take the money from the foundation, slated for the area nonprofits, and use it for personal gain?"

Lucille clung to Garrett all the harder, her face buried in his chest. With a big, protective arm laced around his mother's shoulders, Garrett blinked at the flashbulbs going off and held back the approaching hoard with one hand.

"Don't answer," Hope commanded.

LIKE HE HAD an effing clue what to say. He had no idea what in tarnation the press was referring to.

Out of the corner of his eye, Garrett saw another woman approaching. She was pushing a convertible stroller with a hooded car seat snapped into the top. Dimly aware this was no place for an infant, Garrett turned back to the crowd. His mother looked up at him. "Listen to Hope," Lucille Lockhart hissed.

Like hell he would.

More likely than not, it was Hope Winslow's "management" of the crisis that was turning it into even more of a media circus. Certainly, she'd whipped his mother into a frenzy with her dramatics.

"Of course we didn't take money out of the foundation for our own personal use," he said flatly, watching as Hope signaled vigorously to an airport security guard for help. "Nor do we want to see any area charities fail." That was ridiculous. Especially when his family was set to give away *millions* to those in need.

"But it appears money did not end up in the right hands," another chimed in. "At least not this past year."

"Say the foundation is looking into it," Hope whispered, just loud enough for him to hear.

Ignoring her, he turned back to the reporters and reiterated even more firmly, "No one in my family is a thief."

"So they are just what, then? Irresponsible?" another TV reporter shouted. "Heartless?"

An even more asinine charge. Garrett lifted a staying hand. "That's all I have to say on the matter."

More flashbulbs went off. A contingent of airport security stepped in. They surrounded the reporters, while on the fringes the young woman with the baby resumed her resolute approach. As she neared, Garrett could see it looked as though the young woman had been crying. "Hope! Thank heavens we found you!" the young lady said in a British accent.

Now what? Garrett wondered, exhaling angrily. Was this seemingly heartfelt diversion yet another part of the scandal manager's master plan? Bracing for the answer, he swung back to Hope, eyes narrowing with suspicion. "Who's this?"

Abruptly, Hope looked as tense and on guard as he felt. "Mary Whiting, my nanny," she said.

Chapter Two

Nanny? Hope Winslow had a *nanny*, Garrett thought in shock. And a *baby*?

"Mary? What's going on?" Hope asked in alarm. She dashed around to look inside the covered car seat on top of the combination stroller/buggy. Not surprisingly, Garrett's mother—who longed for grandchildren of her very own—was right by Hope's side.

All Garrett could see from where he stood was the bottom half of a pair of baby blue coveralls, two kicking bootie-clad feet and one tiny hand trying to catch a foot.

Hope's smile was enough to light up the entire world. She bent down to kiss the little hand. Garrett thought, but couldn't be sure, that he heard a happy gurgle in return.

Apparently, all was well. With the infant, anyway, he acknowledged, as his mom stepped back to his side.

Hope put her arm around the young woman. "Has something happened?"

The nanny burst into tears. "It's my mum! She collapsed this morning. They say it's her heart. I've got to go back to England."

Ignoring the inconvenience for her and her child, Hope asked briskly, "Do you have a flight?"

Mary pulled a boarding pass out of her bag. "It leaves in an hour and a half."

Hope sobered. "Then you better get going, if you want to be sure and get through international flight security."

Mary handed over the diaper bag she had looped over one shoulder. "Max's just been fed and burped, and I changed his nappy. Unfortunately, I don't know how long I'll be gone."

Hope nodded. "Take all the time you need…"

"Thank you for understanding!" Mary hugged Hope, gave the cooing baby in the carriage an affectionate pat, then rushed off to catch her flight.

Meanwhile, the reporters were still trying to talk their way past the security guards. Eyeing them, Hope said, "We better get out of here."

Garrett's mom pointed toward the last section of glass doors off the baggage claim. "There's my driver now."

GARRETT HELD THE door while Hope and his mother charged into the Dallas afternoon heat.

His mom entered the limo first and slid across the seat. Hope disengaged the car seat from the stroller and gently set it inside. She followed, more concerned with getting her baby settled and secured than the flash of leg she showed as her skirt rode up her thighs.

Ignoring the immediate hardening of his body, Garrett got in after them. Trying not to let what he had just seen in any way mitigate his initial impression of Hope, he sprawled across the middle of the opposite seat while the two women doted on the baby secured safely between them. "You are such a darling!" Lucille cooed to the baby facing her. "And so alert!" His mother beamed as the infant kicked a blue bootie-clad foot and waved a plump little hand. "How old is he?"

"Twelve weeks on Wednesday," Hope announced proudly. Which meant she was just coming off maternity leave.

Suddenly curious, although he had never actually considered himself a baby person, Garrett asked, "Does the baby have a name?"

Hope's chin lifted. The warmth faded from her eyes. "Max."

Garrett waited for the rest. "Max or Maxwell…?"

Her gaze grew even more wary. "Just Max."

She still hadn't said her son's last name. Nor did she seem about to do so, which made him wonder why.

His mother gave him the kind of look that ordered him to stop fishing around for Hope Winslow's marital status.

Was that what he had been doing? *Maybe*. But who could blame him? He was going to have to know a lot more about Hope Winslow, before he could trust her to handle this crisis for his family.

Satisfied her baby was set for now, Hope turned her glance away from his, pulled her phone out of her bag and quickly checked her messages. "Everything is set up for the press conference," she told his mom.

Not liking the way she seemed ready to cut him out, Garrett asked, "If there's going to be a press conference, why were there reporters at the baggage claim?"

Lucille sighed. "There probably wouldn't have been if I hadn't decided to come and greet you, last minute. The press followed me to the airport."

Hope glanced his way, sunlight streaming in through the window and shimmering in her gilded hair. "They were probably hoping you would be in uniform. Or that you'd say something unfortunate like 'I am not a crook.' Which—by the way—did not even work for Richard Nixon."

He mimicked her droll expression. "You're seriously comparing me to a disgraced politician?"

Hope shrugged in mock innocence.

Lucille looked from Garrett to Hope and back again.

"This is no time to be flirting."

"We're not!" Hope and Garrett said in unison.

Lucille lifted a dissenting brow. "Exactly what I said before I started dating your father."

Garrett felt a flash of grief.

His mom was able to talk freely about his dad, recalling everything about their life together with affection. Not him. Some two and a half years after his dad's passing, thoughts of his late father still left him choked up. Maybe because so much had been left unresolved between them.

Would finally dealing with his inheritance give him the closure he needed?

Hope gave him a long, steady look laced with compassion, then dropped her head and rummaged through her bag. "Let's concentrate on the press conference." She produced the talking points again.

Garrett had been forced into sugarcoating the truth once. He wasn't doing it again. Refusing so much as a cursory glance, he handed Hope her computer tablet back. "Why are you so intent on cleverly orchestrating every word?"

She checked the near constant alerts on her phone as the limo stopped in front of the downtown Dallas high-rise that housed the foundation and numerous elite businesses. With a beleaguered sigh, she predicted, "You'll see."

And he did, as soon as he walked into the elegant ninth floor suite that housed the Lockhart Foundation. A reception area, with a desk and comfortable seating, opened up onto a marble-floored hall that led to four other offices and a boardroom where, he soon discovered, three of his other siblings were waiting.

A collection of laptop computers was spread out on the table. Running on them were clips from every local news station, showing his arrival at the airport, looking grim while declaring his family innocent of all charges, and menacing when his mother turned away from the press and buried her head in his shirt. They even had shots of Max's nanny bursting into tears while approaching Hope, though they didn't say what that was all about.

The longest and most dramatically edited rendition ended with Hope ushering his mother into the limo while looking like a force to be reckoned with. Footage of her baby had been cut. Garrett was happy about that, at least. Her child had no place in this unfolding drama. But there was a shot of him climbing in after the women, just before the door closed, that had him glowering.

The reporter turned back to the camera. "Renowned scandal manager, Hope Winslow, best known for her handling of the crisis involving the American ambassador's son in Great Britain last year, has been retained by the Lockhart family to manage the situation. Which can only mean they are expecting more fireworks to ensue. So stay tuned…"

Looking as stubborn and ornery as the bulls he raised— despite a suit and tie—Garrett's brother, Chance, slapped him on the back and quipped, "Nice job handling the press."

Wyatt also stood, no trace of the horse rancher evident in his sophisticated attire, and gave him a brief hug. Then, grinning wickedly, he agreed, "Articulate, as usual, brother."

His only sister, Sage, in a pretty tailored dress and heels that was very different from her usual cowgirl/chef garb, embraced him warmly. "I don't blame you," she consoled him. "You were caught completely off guard."

Garrett hugged Sage, who'd seemed a little lonesome lately when they talked, and glanced around. Only one Lockhart was missing from their immediate family. His Special Forces brother.

"Zane's out with his unit," Sage informed him.

Which meant no one knew where he was or when he would return.

"In the meantime, we need you to put this on." Hope handed him a garment bag. Inside was a suit and tie, reminiscent of his prep school days.

Thanking heaven they hadn't expected him to wear his army uniform for this sideshow, Garrett rezipped the bag.

"And please…" She took him aside, a delicate hand curving around his arm, and looked him in the eye. "This time, when we assemble before the press, stick to the plan. Say nothing. Just stand in the background, along with the rest of your siblings, and look extremely supportive of your mother."

That, Garrett figured, he could do. At least for now.

When he emerged from the men's room, still tying his tie, there was a team there, doing hair and makeup.

"Don't even think about it," he growled when they tried to put powder on him. His brothers were equally resistant.

Hope stood nearby, her baby in her arms, sizing him up.

He wondered if she was that observant when she made love. And why the notion that she might be was so sexy.

But there was no more time to think about it, because Hope was giving his mother one last pep talk, and then it was show time. After handing her baby off to Sharla, his mother's executive assistant, Hope and the family took the elevator down to another floor and filed into the meeting room reserved for the occasion, where two dozen members of the press were already assembled.

His mother stepped up to the microphone. "Thank you all for coming. Like you, we have been shocked and alarmed to hear allegations that not all of the funds from the Lockhart Foundation have been sent as promised to the local organizations we assist. We haven't yet been able to ver-

ify what has actually happened but we are looking into
the matter."

"You seem skeptical that any payments were missed,"
a reporter looking for a more salacious story observed.

From the front row, where she was seated, Garrett could
see Hope shaking her head, wordlessly warning his mother
not to answer.

But Lucille could not remain silent when her integrity
was in question. "I admit I don't see how it could have happened, when I signed all those checks myself."

At that, it was all Garrett could do not to groan. His
mother had just announced she was personally liable for
whatever had happened.

"And yet there are now—at last count," the chief inves-
tigative reporter from the *Dallas Sun News* said, "*sixteen*
charities claiming they've been shorted. It's pretty suspi-
cious that all those groups would be claiming the same
thing, don't you think?"

Sixteen, Garrett thought, stunned. Just a few hours ago,
when Hope had shown him the talking points on her tablet, it had been *three*.

Hope got up gracefully to her feet and moved across
the row to the aisle.

"Why isn't the Lockhart Foundation's chief financial
officer, Paul Smythe, answering any of our questions?"
another correspondent asked.

"He's out of town on a personal matter," Lucille said
calmly. "When he returns, we'll get to the bottom of this."

"And if you don't?" another journalist pressed, as Hope
glided onto the stage. "Are you prepared to fire Mr. Smythe
and/or anyone else involved in what increasingly looks like a
severe misappropriation—if not downright embezzlement—
of funds?"

His mom faltered.

Hope took the microphone. "Now, Tom, you know as well as I do that's premature, given that nothing has been confirmed yet…"

With grudging admiration, Garrett watched Hope field a few more questions and then pleasantly end the conference with the promise of another update just as soon as they had information to share.

"So what's next?" he asked when the family had reassembled in the foundation quarters.

Hope lifted Max into her arms, cuddling him close, then looked at Lucille. "We move on to Step 2 of our scandal-management plan."

"DID YOU VOLUNTEER to drive us out to Laramie County? Or were you drafted?" Hope demanded two hours later, when Garrett Lockhart landed on the doorstep of her comfortable suburban Dallas home.

She already knew he wasn't gung ho about the plan to have his mother stay at the Circle H, the family's ranch in rural west Texas, to get her out of the limelight until they could figure out what was going on with the foundation.

Garrett shrugged. Clad in a blue shirt, jeans and boots, with the hint of an evening beard rimming his jaw, he looked sexy and totally at ease. "Does it matter?"

Yes, oddly enough, it did matter whether he was helping because he wanted to or because he had been forced to do so. "Just curious."

He flashed a half smile. "Combination of the two."

It was like pulling mud out of a pit. "Care to explain?" Hope directed him and his duffel bag to the driveway, where a ton of gear sat, ready to be loaded into the back of her sporty red SUV.

He fit his bag into the left side, where she pointed. "Given how we feel about each other, a three-plus hour journey locked in the same vehicle is bound to be a little awkward."

No kidding. Hope set a pack-n-play on top of his bag. "Then why bother?"

He lifted her suitcase and set it next to his. "I don't have a vehicle of my own to drive right now, and I won't until I get to Laramie County and can borrow a pickup from one of my brothers. Going with you will save me the hassle of renting a car here."

"You could have ridden with your mother and her chauffeur."

Arms folded in front of him, he lounged to one side. "Not going to happen."

She slid him a glance, wishing he didn't look so big and strong and immovable. "Why not?"

His gaze roved her knee-length khaki shorts and red notch-collared blouse before returning to her face. "Because I don't want to spend the entire journey dodging questions I don't want to answer."

His lazy quip brought heat to her cheeks. "Hint, hint?"

"If the shoe fits…"

Boy, he was maddening.

Worse, she didn't know why she was letting him get under her skin. She dealt with difficult people all the time.

Maybe they weren't six feet five inches tall and handsome as all get-out, and military-grade sexy, but…still…

Aware he was watching her, gauging her reactions as carefully as she was checking out his, she lifted her chin. "What were the other reasons?"

This time he grinned. Big time. "It'll save me from leading the search party later."

Knowing a thinly veiled insult when she heard one, Hope scowled. "*What* search party?"

"The one that's sent out to find you and your baby in the wilds of Laramie County when you get lost after dark."

Hope inhaled deeply. Breathed out slowly. Gave him one of her trademark *watch it* looks. "I think I can read a map, *Captain*."

"No doubt, sweetheart," he said in a droll tone. "But unless you can telepathically figure out which road is which when you come to an unmarked intersection in the Middle of Nowhere, West Texas…you might want to rethink that."

Being lost with a baby who needed to be fed and diapered every few hours was not her ideal scenario, either. "Fine." She gave him a warning glance. "But you're driving so I can work."

He took the keys. "Wouldn't have it any other way. My only question is—" Garrett eyed the pile of luggage and baby gear still sitting in her driveway "—can you and/or your *significant other* load the car?"

There he went with the questions about her private life again. Although, why it would matter to him she had no idea. But to save both of them a great big headache, she figured she might as well be blunt.

"First of all, there is no significant other," she retorted, and thought—but couldn't be sure—that she saw a flash of something in his blue eyes as she continued expertly packing the cargo compartment with the rest of her gear. "Second, it's not that much stuff." She went into the house and returned, toting a sound-asleep Max—who was already belted into his safety seat—to the roomy SUV. Garrett watched her lock Max's carrier into its base in the center of the rear seat.

"If you say so."

Clearly, he still had something on his mind.

Hope straightened. "What is it?"

"I'm all for getting my mother out of the public eye. But

are you sure this is going to work? Property records are public. The press could still figure out where she's gone."

Hope appreciated his concern for his family's welfare. "They could."

"But…?"

"It's unlikely a Dallas news crew will travel three hours out to Laramie, and then back, just to hear a *no comment* from someone other than your mother. When they could easily interview someone from a nonprofit right here in the metroplex who has a lot to say about how they and the people they serve have been wronged."

"You're the scandal manager." Garrett settled behind the wheel, his large, muscular frame filling up the interior of her car. Frowning, he fit the key into the ignition. "But can't you pressure the news organizations to present *both* sides of the story?"

"Yes, and for the record, I already have." Hope climbed into the passenger seat and closed the garage via remote. "But the Dallas papers and TV stations can still keep the story going—and ostensibly show your side, too—although not necessarily in a positive light."

His brow furrowed at her careful tone. "How, if my mother isn't available for any more interviews?"

Nor was anyone else in the family, Hope knew, since his only sister, Sage, was already en route back to Seattle, to handle a catering gig the next day. Chance and Wyatt were headed back to their West Texas ranches, to care for their herds. And Garrett had certainly made it clear he didn't intend to cooperate with the press. She exhaled. "The media can show old news footage of your mother and father when they announced the formation of the Lockhart Foundation."

Garrett's shoulders tensed. "That was a black-tie gala."

"Right. And would likely be salaciously depicted, at least by some outlets, as the Haves versus the Have Nots."

Garrett slid a pair of sunglasses on over his eyes. "So, in other words, we're damned if we stay and have reporters chasing after us with every new accusation. And damned if we leave town and avoid their inquiries, too."

"Not for long, if I do my job, which I certainly plan to do."

To Hope's relief, for the first time since they'd met, he seemed willing to let her take charge of the volatile situation. At least temporarily. So, while Garrett drove, she worked on her laptop computer and her infant son slept.

It was only when they entered rural Laramie County, near dusk, that the trip took an eventful turn.

"Do you see that?" Hope pointed to a disabled pickup truck ahead. The hood was up on the battered vehicle. A young couple stood beside the smoking engine, apparently as unhappy with each other as they were with their transportation.

Worse, the young man—with a muscular upper body and military haircut—was on crutches, his left leg obscured by pressure bandages and a complicated brace.

Garrett drove up beside them. "Need a helping hand?"

"I'm Darcy Dunlop," the young woman said, her thin face lighting up with relief. "And yes!"

"We've got it." Her grim-faced companion shook his head.

"Tank!" Darcy said, wringing her hands in distress.

"We'll just wait for the tow truck."

"But the mechanic said we didn't have to be here! As long as we leave the truck unlocked, he can take it back to the garage in town on his own."

Tank's jaw set, even more stubbornly.

Garrett stuck out his hand, introducing himself. "Army Medical Corps…"

The other man's expression relaxed slightly. "Infantry. Until this." He pointed to his injured leg. "Not sure what I'm going to do next…"

They talked a little about the fellow soldier who had saved Tank's life, and the IED fragments that had made a mess of his limb. How his parents—who lived locally—had taken them in during the year it was going to take to recover and get his strength back.

"That's rough," Garrett said in commiseration.

Darcy's lower lip trembled. "What's worse is how far we have to go so Tank can get treatment. We either drive back and forth to the closest military hospital—which is a couple hours from here—or Tank gets his care in Laramie. And the rehab there, well, I mean everybody's nice, but they have no experience with what's happened to Tank."

Garrett understood—as did Hope—that there were some things only fellow soldiers, who had served in a war zone, could comprehend. The camaraderie was as essential to healing as medical care. Garrett gave Tank a look of respect. "How about we give you a lift home."

Darcy gave her husband a pleading look.

Shoulders slumping in relief, the former soldier consented. "Thanks."

Knowing Tank would have more room for his leg brace in the front, Hope climbed in back to sit with Max, who was beginning to wake up. Darcy took the other side. The two women chatted while Tank gave directions to his parents' home, a few miles north.

When they arrived, Garrett scribbled a number on the back of a business card and handed it to the other man. "I'll be around for the next few days, taking care of some family business, so if you need anything…"

Tank shook his hand. "Appreciate it."

Hope could see the meeting had affected Garrett. It had affected her, too.

"I don't understand how the military can boot someone out, just because they got injured," she fumed, as they drove away.

Garrett paused to study the unmarked intersection of country roads. No street names were showing up on her GPS screen, Hope noted. Which meant she might, indeed, have gotten lost trying to find her way to the ranch.

"It was probably his choice to get a medical discharge rather than stay in," Garrett pointed out, pausing to glance at a set of directions he had in his pocket, before turning south again.

"Why would Tank do that when he clearly loved being part of the armed service?"

"Because doing so would have meant taking a desk job, once he had recuperated, and my guess is Tank didn't see himself being happy that way. He probably wanted to be with his buddies—who were all still in Infantry—or out of the service completely," he said, as they reached the entrance to the Circle H Ranch.

Hope wasn't sure what she had expected, since Lucille had promised they would all be quite comfortable there, and have as much privacy as they needed. Maybe something as luxurious as Lucille's Dallas mansion. But the turnoff was marked by a mailbox, and a wrought-iron sign that had definitely seen better days. The gravel lane leading up to the ranch house was bordered by a fence that was falling down in places. The barn and stables looked just as dilapidated.

Garrett cut the engine.

Handsome face taut with concern, he got out and opened

the door for her. "Mom and her driver were supposed to be here ahead of us."

Obviously, that had not happened. Max, who'd been remarkably quiet and content, let out an impatient cry.

"I know, baby," Hope soothed, patting her son on the back. "You're hungry. Probably wet, too." She lifted him out of the car seat and moved to stand beside Garrett. "But we're going to take care of all that."

Garrett led her up onto the porch of the rambling two-story ranch house with the gabled roof. He unlocked the door and swung it open. Like him, Hope could only stare.

Chapter Three

The interior of the ranch house had not been updated in decades, was devoid of all furniture and was scrupulously clean. In deference to the closed window blinds, Garrett hit switches as he moved through the four wood-paneled downstairs rooms. Sighing, he noted, "Well, at least all the lights work."

"Does the air conditioning work?" she asked, their footsteps echoing on the scarred pine floors. It was much hotter inside the domicile than outside. And the outside was at least ninety degrees, even as the sun was setting.

"No clue." Garrett headed upstairs. There were only two bedrooms. One bath. No beds. Or even a chair for Hope to sit in while she nursed.

They headed back downstairs, Max still fussing. Worse, she could feel her breasts beginning to leak in response. "When was the last time you were here?" Glad she'd thought to put soft cotton nursing pads inside her bra, she opened up the diaper bag she'd slung over her arm and pulled out a blanket.

Garrett stepped out onto the back porch, where a porch swing looked out over the property. "Ah—never."

Deciding her son had waited long enough, Hope sat down on the swing and situated Max in her arms. Waving at Garrett to turn around, which he obediently did, she unbuttoned her blouse and unsnapped the front of her nursing bra. Max found her nipple and latched on hungrily. "I was under the impression this was family property." She shifted her son more comfortably in her arms and draped the blanket over him. As he fed, they both relaxed. "That your mother grew up on the Circle H."

"She did." Hands in his pockets, Garrett continued looking over the property, which was quite beautiful in a wild, untamed way. Overgrown shrubbery, dotted with blossoms, filled the air with a lush, floral scent.

He studied the sun disappearing slowly beneath the horizon in a streaky burst of yellow and red. "But she and my dad sold the place after my grandfather Henderson's death, when she was twenty-three. They used the proceeds to start Dad's hedge fund and stake their life in Dallas."

It was a move that had certainly paid off for Frank and Lucille Lockhart. They'd made millions. Hope turned her attention to the collection of buildings a distance away from the house. A couple of barns with adjacent corrals and a rambling one-story building with cedar siding and a tin roof. Maybe a bunkhouse? "When did the property come back into the family?"

Garrett reached down and plucked out a long weed sprouting through the bushes and tossed it aside. "My dad bought it for my mom as an anniversary gift the year he sold his company so he could retire. They were going to fix the ranch up as a retreat. He purchased property in Laramie County for all five of us kids, too. So we'd all have a tangible link to our parents' history here."

Hope shifted Max to her other breast, glad they had the light from the interior of the house illuminating the porch with a soft yellow glow now that it was beginning to get dark. It was just enough to allow her to see what she was doing and yet afford her some privacy, too.

"I gather your dad also grew up in West Texas?"

Garrett nodded, his handsome profile brooding yet calm as he surveyed the sagebrush, live oak trees and cedars dotting the landscape. "On the Wind River Ranch, here in Laramie County. My parents bought that back, too. My brother Wyatt started a horse farm there."

Max nursed quickly—a sign of just how hungry he'd been. When he was done, Hope shifted her sated son upright so he could burp, and used her other hand to refasten her nursing bra. "So you all have ranches then."

"No." Garrett paced the length of the porch, both hands shoved in the back pockets of his jeans. The action drew her attention to his masculine shoulders and spectacularly muscled flanks. Without warning, she recalled the feel of his rock-hard leg beneath her palm, the heat radiating from the apex of his thighs. Wondered what it would be like to be held against all that sheer male power and strength.

Then she pushed the disturbing notion away.

Oblivious to the lusty direction of her thoughts, he paced a little farther away. "My dad gifted me a house and a medical office building in town." He chuckled when Max let out a surprisingly loud belch.

"It's okay. I'm done," Hope said.

Garrett turned to face her. Noting she had rebuttoned her blouse, he ambled toward her once again. "Sage received a small café in the historic downtown section of Laramie and the apartment above it."

Hope spread the blanket out on the seat of the swing and laid Max down so she could change his diaper. "So you'd all eventually settle here?"

He moved even closer, gazing fondly down at her sleepy baby. The tenderness in his gaze was a surprise.

"That was their plan," he admitted in a voice so gentle it made her mouth go dry.

She drew in a breath for calm. Which, to her consternation, did not help.

She still was wa-a-a-a-y too aware of him. Still far too curious about the man who was proving to be such an enigma—all Texas military gentleman one moment, all tough, edgy alpha male the next. Telling herself to dial it down a notch, Hope cocked her head. "What's your plan?" she asked bluntly.

His gaze dipped to her lips, lingered. "To sell both properties and move on."

"Your mom said your tour of duty was about up."

"Twenty-nine days. I saved my time off for the end, so I'm on R & R through the rest of it."

"And then…?"

"I either reenlist and become a staff physician at Walter Reed in Washington, DC…"

She could see him doing that. And probably loving it. "Or…?"

"Head up a residency program at a hospital in Seattle."

"Where your sister Sage is living."

He nodded.

She could imagine him teaching, too. Having all the young female residents fall hopelessly in love with him. "Do you know what you're going to do?"

"Still thinking about it."

"But in either case you won't be returning to Texas." As his mother wanted.

His sharp, assessing gaze met hers. "No."

"Not tied to the Lone Star State in any way?" Despite the fact he and his siblings had apparently all grown up in Texas.

He raised his brows. "Are you?"

Hope nodded, her heart tightening a little in her chest. "I've worked in enough places to realize Texas is my home. And where I want Max to grow up."

Feeling oddly disappointed that it was a sentiment they obviously did not share, and at the same time determined to end the unexpected intimacy that had fallen between them, she finished diapering her son, then lifted Max into her arms. "Where are we going to bunk down tonight?" she asked, shooting Garrett an all-business look. "I assume your mom had some definitive plan when she suggested we come out here. Maybe a hotel in town, assuming there is one?"

Garrett reached for his cell phone. "I'll give my mother a call, see if I can find out what her ETA is."

Hope headed to the SUV to get Max settled in his infant seat, so they would be ready to lock up the house and go wherever they were headed next as soon as he got off the phone. To her relief, her little boy, exhausted from the chaotic activity of the day, was already fast asleep when Garrett came out of the house, informing her, "We've been directed to the bunkhouse."

Why did she suddenly have the feeling that was not a good thing? Hope stood, her hands propped on her hips. "When will everyone else be here?"

His expression as matter-of-fact as his low tone, he answered, "Noon tomorrow."

HOPE BLINKED. SHE could not have heard right! "Noon *tomorrow*?"

"My mother decided to stay in Dallas and handle some things there first."

"Unlike me, you don't seem all that surprised."

He narrowed his eyes. "What are you accusing me of?"

She flushed. "Nothing." She just knew that being alone with this sexy, virile man was not a good idea. "But," she continued hastily, "under the circumstances, I think it would be better if Max and I went into town and stayed in a hotel."

He choked off a laugh. "What? You're worried I'm going to put the moves on you?"

Actually, she was worried *she* was going to lose all common sense and put the moves on him. But not about to reveal that, she crossed her arms in front of her and quipped wryly, "Dream on, Alpha Man."

His eyes crinkled mischievously at the corners. *"Alpha Man?"*

Had she really *said* that? She must be punchier than she'd thought. Which was par for the course, considering she'd been lured back to work three months before she had planned and then, compounding matters, having to get up at the crack of dawn to take the six o'clock flight from Dallas to DC in order to be seated next to him on the return trip. Aware he was still waiting for an explanation, she lifted a hand. "It was an insult. A friendly one." Hope bit down on an oath. She was just making it worse.

He laughed, his husky baritone like music to her ears, as he continued giving her a long, sexy once-over. "Sounded more like a compliment to me."

He was twisting everything around, embarrassing her and putting her off her game. Indignant, she huffed, "Of course you would think that."

He held his ground, arms folded in front of him, biceps bunched. Again, that long steady appraisal. "Because I'm alpha?"

He definitely was *not* a beta.

She threaded her hands through her hair, wishing she'd thought to put it in a tight, spinsterish bun before he'd picked her up. "Can we end this repartee?"

His mother was right. They had been flirting. They were flirting now. Heaven help them both.

He leaned in and gathered her into his arms. "With pleasure."

The feel of him against her, chest to chest, thigh to thigh, sucked all the remaining air from her lungs.

"What are you doing?" she gasped, wishing he didn't feel so very, very good.

Wishing he hadn't just reminded her of all that had been missing from her life.

He threaded his hand through her hair, let it settle tenderly on the nape of her neck. "What any alpha male would do in this situation." Grinning, he bent his head toward hers.

Hope tingled all over. Lower still, there was a kindling warmth. Cursing the forbidden excitement welling within her, she whispered, "Garrett...for pity's sake...you can't... *I can't...*!"

He laughed again, even more wickedly. His lips hovered above hers, so close their breaths were meeting as sensually and irrevocably as the rest of them.

"Kiss you and see if you kiss me back?" he taunted softly, stroking the pad of his thumb along the curve of her lips—top, then bottom. "Oh, yes, Hope Winslow, I sure as hell can."

Not only can, Hope thought, as an avalanche of excitement roared through her. Did.

His lips fit over hers, coaxingly at first, then with more and more insistence. She told herself to resist. Tried to resist. But her treacherous body refused to listen to her heart, which had been wounded, and her mind, which absolutely knew better.

She had been alone for so long.

Had needed to be touched, held, for months now.

She hadn't expected to be cherished as if she were the most wonderful woman on Earth. But that was exactly what he was doing, as he stroked his hand through her hair and, with his other palm flattened against her spine, guided her closer until her breasts were pressed against the unyielding hardness of his chest. Lower still, she felt the heat in his thighs and the building desire. And knew her life had just begun to get hopelessly complicated...

GARRETT HADN'T COME out to the ranch thinking they would be alone for one single second. Hadn't figured he would ever act on the need that had consumed him since the second her bottom landed square on his lap, the softness of her breasts pushing into his face.

Oh, he'd known he wanted her from the instant he had seen her checking him out in the DC airport. She was just so gorgeous, so haughty and unreachable in that all-business way of hers.

Seeing she had an infant whom she cared deeply for, knowing she was irrevocably wedded to life in Texas while he was not, had added yet another reason he should keep his hands off.

He might have managed it, too, if she hadn't been working so hard to curtail the attraction she so obviously felt.

Because Hope was right about one thing. Her denial had brought out the alpha male in him. Made him want to pursue her like she had never been pursued before.

That pursuit, in turn, had kindled his own raging desire. And then she had kissed him back, her tongue entwined with his in a way that could bring him to his knees and one day, hopefully, land them both in bed.

Luckily for the two of them she came to her senses and pushed him away. Breathing raggedly, she stepped back, a gut-wrenching turmoil in her low tone he hadn't expected. "I can't do this."

Pressing her hand to her kiss-swollen lips, she shook her head. "I can't lose everything because of one reckless moment. *Not again.*"

SILENCE FELL BETWEEN THEM, as awful and wrenching as her voice. Mortified, Hope yanked open her car door and climbed behind the wheel.

Garrett walked to the passenger side and pulled himself in beside her. "When did that happen?"

Hope concentrated on starting the engine. Driving, the normalcy of it, would help. She looked behind her, then backed up until she reached the gravel road that led to the barns. "I shouldn't have said that."

"And I shouldn't have kissed you," Garrett admitted gruffly, his big body filling up the passenger compartment the way no one else ever had. "But now that I did, and you kissed me back…"

He shrugged like a soldier on leave.

As if the fact that he had just returned from a war zone entitled him to something. Namely, a woman willing to have a fling.

She had found out the hard way, however, through her ill-advised liaison with Max's daddy, that woman was not her.

"That shouldn't have happened, either," she said stiffly, as the SUV wound past the damaged wooden fence to the lone building a distance away from everything.

She didn't have to guess what it was.

A sign next to the door of the cedar-sided, tin-roofed building said Circle H Ranch Bunkhouse.

A bright red welcome mat stood in front of the heavy wooden door. Pots of flowers, a couple of small tables and some rough-hewn Adirondack chairs decorated the front porch. Lamps, emitting a soft yellow glow on either side of the entry had been turned on.

If the inviting exterior was any indication of the inside of the domicile, then Lucille had been right, they would be comfortable here.

Hope cut the engine and got out of the car. Quietly, she opened the rear passenger door, unfastened Max's safety seat from the base of the restraint and lifted him out. To her relief, her sweet little boy slept blissfully on.

Garrett grabbed the diaper bag and went on ahead, to find the key that had been left beneath the mat. "Is all this because you're working for my mother?" He reached inside and switched the interior lights on.

"Believe it or not—" Hope squared her shoulders as she passed "—working for your mother doesn't include making out with you."

GARRETT WAS PRETTY sure Hope hadn't meant to say that. Any more than she'd meant to do anything she had the last fifteen minutes or so. Nevertheless, he was pleased to see her letting down her guard. He wanted to get to know the real Hope Winslow, not the sophisticated facade she showed the world.

He watched as she set the carrier holding her sleeping infant down. "I won't interfere with that. Well, no more than I would have, anyway."

She smiled at him as if they hadn't just brought each other's bodies roaring back to life. "Good to know, Captain."

Together, they took a quick tour of the newly renovated bunkhouse.

The central part of the structure included an open-concept kitchen with a breakfast bar that looked out onto the great room, complete with a TV and U-shaped sofa and a large plank table with a dozen chairs plus an arm chair on each end. On each side of it was a hallway that led to three bedrooms. All six bedrooms were outfitted identically, with a queen-sized bed, desk, dresser and private bath. His mom had been right, Garrett noted. They all could be very comfortable here.

Except for the awareness simmering between Hope and him…

"I don't understand why you think it would matter if we did become…closer. I'm not the one employing you— my mother is."

Hope sighed, apparently appreciating his use of the least offensive word he could think of. "It would still look bad."

"And that concerns you, how things look?"

"Yes." Stepping closer, she slid him a surprised glance. "Doesn't it concern you?"

He exhaled his exasperation. "Not really. Something is either right or it's wrong. What we just experienced felt very right."

Hope turned away as if they hadn't just shared an embrace that had rocked his world. "It doesn't matter," she said, as if to a four-year-old. "Scandal management is all about appearances."

Ah, *appearances*. The bane of his youth.

He moved close enough to see the frustration glimmering in her eyes.

Her elegant features tinged an emotional pink, she said, "I just started my own firm. Your mother's scandal is the first crisis I'm handling, solo. It has to go well."

Of course business came first with her.

"Or?"

She sighed, completely vulnerable now as she met his gaze, seeming on the verge of tears. "Or my reputation really will be ruined."

That was almost as hard to believe as the way he was suddenly feeling about her, as if she might just be worth sticking around for. He moved closer yet. Seeing it *was* a tear trembling just beneath her lower lash, he lifted a thumb, gently brushed it away. "Over one job?" And one very long, satisfying kiss that had led him to want so much more?

She swallowed, stepped back. The tenderness he felt for her doubled.

"I made a mistake when I was working for my previous employer."

He couldn't imagine it being as calamitous as she was making it out to be. It was all he could do not to take her back in his arms. "What happened?"

For a second he thought she wouldn't answer, then she apparently thought better of it—maybe because she knew in this day and age almost anything could be researched on the internet.

Hope turned and walked back out to her SUV. She lifted out the pack-n-play, handed it off to him, then pulled out a box of diapers and a bag of baby necessities. "I got involved with a British journalist reporting on a scandal involving the American ambassador's son. Nothing happened between us during the crisis. But there was a flirtation that later turned into a love affair."

He grabbed her suitcase and headed up the steps alongside her. No wonder she'd reacted the way she had when his mother accused them of flirting. "I'm guessing it ended badly?"

Hope set her things down in the bedroom farthest from the living area. She opened up the pack-n-play, erecting it quickly. "I wanted marriage and a family. Lyle didn't. So we broke up. A few weeks later, he was killed in a motorcycle accident while on vacation with another woman. A couple of weeks after that, I discovered I was pregnant with Max."

Although he felt bad for all she'd been through, he realized he liked her better like this, showing her more vulnerable side.

"Sounds rough. But you were happy about the pregnancy?"

Hope smiled softly, glowing a little at the memory. "I was over the moon."

He could see that. And it was easy to understand why. She had a great kid.

Hope stroked a hand through her honey-gold hair. "My bosses, however, were not anywhere near as ecstatic."

Hope went back to put a soft cotton sheet over the crib mattress. She bent over, tucking in the elastic edges, while he stood by, watching, knowing she had no idea just how beautiful she was, never mind what she could do to a man, just by being, breathing…

She straightened, her green eyes serious, as she looked up at him. "My superiors worried, even though I had already arranged for a nanny from a topflight agency to assist me, that a baby would interfere with my ability to manage crises."

Her teeth raked her plump lower lip, reminding him just how passionately she kissed. "Plus, they were upset about the rumors started by some of my rivals that hinted I'd leaked confidential information to Lyle Loddington, prior to our affair. It wasn't true. I never disclosed even a smidgen of confidential information about anything to him. But you know how people think, where there's love, there is pillow talk…"

Pillow talk with her would have to be amazing. Not to mention everything that came before it.

With effort, he forced his mind back to the conversation. "So your employer fired you?"

"I was asked to resign."

It was easy to see that still stung. He got angry on her behalf. "You could have fought it."

He followed her back outside to the rear of her SUV. Together, they carried what was left of their luggage inside. "Yes," she agreed, "but if I had I would have done even more damage to my reputation in the process." He shut the door quietly behind them. "So I decided to use what I had learned and start my own firm—which would allow me to control the timing and length of my maternity leave—and go back to work when Max was six months old."

"Which would have been three months from now."

"Right. And I'm happy with that decision, even though I was persuaded to return to work a little earlier than I had planned. I *like* the way my life is shaping up, Garrett."

Able to see she didn't want to do anything to jeopardize that, he took her hand. "I'm sorry you had such a tough time." Crazy as it sounded, he wished he had been there to support and protect her. To help her though whatever upheaval she'd had to face. It's not something anyone should have to go through alone.

Her expression grew stony with resolve. "It was my fault. I was reckless. But I'm not going to be reckless again."

Chapter Four

"You're not planning to go back to work now, are you?" Garrett asked, a short while later. He opened up the fridge that had been stocked by the bunkhouse caretaker in advance of their arrival, brought out a big stack of deli meats and cheeses and laid them out on the concrete kitchen countertop, next to an assortment of bakery goods.

Hope set her laptop and phone down on the breakfast bar just long enough to grab a small bunch of green grapes and pour herself a tall glass of milk.

"No choice." Ignoring his look of concern, she settled on a tall stool opposite him. Ten thirty at night or not, she had business to conduct. And she needed to do it while her son was sound asleep. "I have to check the message boards for the news outlets reporting on the scandal, to see how the news thus far is being received."

Garrett spread both sides of a multigrain roll with spicy brown mustard, then layered on lettuce, tomato, ham, turkey and cheddar cheese. "There's nothing you can do about the way people think."

"Au contraire, Captain Lockhart."

He grinned.

Too late, she realized that flip remark had been a mistake.

He thought she was flirting with him again. And she definitely. Was. Not.

Hope turned her attention back to the task at hand. Her mood flatlined.

"That bad?"

Hope grimaced. "Worse than I expected and I expected it to be…bad."

"Hit me with the highlights," he said, twisting the cap off a beer.

Clearing her throat, she read, "'Those Lockharts should all be put in jail—'"

"We have not done anything illegal."

But someone might have, Hope knew. "'The whole foundation should be shut down…'" she continued.

Flicking a glance her way, Garrett crossed his arms over his chest. Fresh out of the shower, in a pair of gray running shorts and T-shirt stamped Army, he looked relaxed. And sexy as hell. "An overreaction."

Hitching in a quavering breath, Hope turned back to the article and recited, "'Why do the rich always feel the need to steal from the poor?'"

A ghost of a smile crossed his mouth. "I'm detecting a theme."

"This is serious."

Ever alert, he shrugged. "It's just people spouting off on the internet."

"Someone in the family needs to respond."

He ripped open a bag of chips and offered it to her. "And I'm the logical choice?"

She waved them off and ate a grape instead. "You *are* the eldest son, the patriarch, since your father passed."

He carried his plate around the counter and set it in front of a stool. "And I will make a public statement." He dropped down beside her, swiveled so he was facing her. "Once we have all the facts."

Their knees were almost touching but it would have

been a sign of weakness on her part to move back. "You know why some politicians or businesses in trouble survive and others don't?"

His eyes on her, he took another sip of beer.

"Because they know every time an allegation is made, no matter how outlandish, a response must be given."

"Nothing makes a person look guiltier than constantly proclaiming they aren't."

"So I take it that's a no?"

"That's a no," he said, and devoured his sandwich.

With a sigh, she went back to her computer, logged on to the message boards for the news story with the most harmful coverage, and began to type.

Finished, he edged closer. "What are you doing?"

"Responding."

He stood behind her, so he could look over her shoulder. "Under your own name?"

Oh, my, he smelled good. Like soap and shampoo and man. "Under a fictitious screen name I set up. One of many."

"Isn't that…?"

She cut him off before he could say dishonest. "The way things are done today, and yes, it is."

He watched her fingers fly across the keyboard, then read aloud, "'What ever happened to being innocent until proven guilty? The Lockhart family has magnanimously supported over one hundred metroplex charities over the last thirty-five years. I say give them a chance to find out what has happened, before we all pass judgment.'"

Garrett returned to his stool. "Nice."

Seconds later, another Internet post appeared.

Hope shifted her laptop screen, so he could see. He read again, "'I agree with #1HotDallasMama. We *should* wait and see…'"

Several more posts appeared. Two out of three were positive.

Resisting the urge to do a touchdown dance, Hope turned to Garrett. "See?"

He polished off his chips, one at a time. "So that worked. Until someone puts up another negative rant, then other message-boarders are apt to agree with *their* posts."

Hope sighed her exasperation. "The point is to get another view out there. Repeatedly, if necessary, until the facts come in, and we can respond accordingly."

"Another press conference?"

"Or interview and statement."

She was not surprised to find he wasn't looking forward to any of it.

Telling herself that it didn't matter what Garrett Lockhart thought of her methods or her job, she carried her dishes to the sink. Turned, only to find Garrett was right beside her, doing the same thing. She looked up. He looked down. She had the strong sensation he was tempted to kiss her again. And she might have let him, had Max not let out a fierce cry. Thank heaven, Hope thought, pivoting quickly to attend to her maternal duties, her son had more sense than she appeared to right now.

"WHERE DO YOU want all these files?" Garrett asked his mother when she arrived at the bunkhouse late the following morning, Paul Smythe's daughter, Adelaide Smythe, in tow. A certified public accountant and forensic auditor, as well as an old family friend, the young woman had agreed to help them sort through the records and try to piece together what had happened.

Appearing tired but determined, Lucille pointed to the big plank table in the main room. "Just put them all there, thanks," she said.

Garrett set the boxes down, then returned to Adelaide's minivan to bring in the rest.

"When are you due?" Hope asked the visibly pregnant Adelaide.

"Four and a half months. I know—" Adelaide ran a hand over her rounded belly "—it looks like I'm a little further along, but it's because I'm having twins."

"Who's the lucky daddy?" Garrett asked, wondering how his brother Wyatt was going to take the news. The two had dated seriously in high school, but been extraordinarily contentious toward each other ever since they broke up at the end of their senior year. Why, exactly, no one knew. Just that there was still a lot of emotion simmering there.

"Donor number 19867." A beaming Adelaide explained, "I conceived the new-fashioned way."

Garrett wasn't surprised Adelaide had opted for pregnancy via sperm bank; she always had been very independent.

Hope sorted the multihued folders according to the names on the files. "Speaking of fathers...any luck getting ahold of your dad?"

Adelaide set up two laptop computers and a portable printer. "We're still trying, but he's apparently *not* on his annual fly fishing and camping trip in the wilds of Montana with the guys."

"Then where is he?" Garrett asked with a frown.

Adelaide glanced at Lucille, who seemed both understanding and sympathetic. Reluctantly, she admitted, "He's probably on vacation with this lady exec he's been secretly dating."

Hope tilted her head, her long, honey-hued hair falling over her shoulders. "Why secretly?"

Garrett itched to drag his hands through her lustrous mane, draw her close...

Adelaide sighed loudly. "Because I didn't like Mirabelle the first time I met her. I thought she was a gold digger, and I made the mistake of telling my dad that." She grimaced, recollecting. "Anyway, the whole thing got so ugly, we agreed not to talk about it ever again. So if my dad is on vacation with Mirabelle, as Lucille and I both suspect, he's probably not looking at his phone much at all."

Garrett could understand that. There were times when he wanted to get away from it all and enjoy the company of a woman, too. Like now...

"But he can never be disconnected from the world for too long, so we expect to hear from him soon." Adelaide plugged in power cords.

"Any idea what happened regarding the missing or misappropriated funds yet?" Garrett asked.

Again, Adelaide shook her head. "All we've managed to do thus far is gather all the records in one place. Which isn't as easy as it sounds, because there were some at the foundation office, some at Lucille's, some at Dad's house." She surveyed the stacks upon stacks of files. "We'll put it all together, but the actual audit is going to take a while."

"How long?" Hope asked.

"A couple of days."

She looked unhappy about that. "What can we do to help speed things along?"

His mother consulted the lengthy handwritten to-do list in her leather notebook. "You and Garrett could go into town. Talk with the director of the nonprofit the foundation is funding there." Lucille wrote out the information, handed it over. "If the foundation has indeed let down Bess Monroe and the wounded warriors she is trying to help, it's going to take both of you to fix things."

"THIS CAN'T BE RIGHT." Hope paused in front of the door to Monroe's Western Wear clothing store, Lucille's notes in hand. Yet the street address matched, as did the last names.

Garrett, who had decided to carry Max in lieu of getting the stroller out of the SUV, said, "Let's go in and see."

A young man behind the counter approached. "Can I help you?" he asked.

Briefly, they explained the problem. "I'm Nick Monroe. Bess's brother," the genial dark-haired man explained. "Bess is using our family store as the nonprofit's address because she doesn't yet have the funds for a facility."

"We'd like to talk to her."

"She's just about to get off shift at the hospital where she works." Nick Monroe paused. "Although I'm not sure how happy she is going to be to see you-all. She's not too happy with the Lockhart Foundation these days."

An understatement, as it turned out.

Although her shift had officially ended by the time they arrived at the rehab department, Bess Monroe was still deep in conversation with a little girl in a back brace and the girl's mother. The rest of the well-equipped physical therapy clinic was filled with all ages and injuries, including a couple of people who appeared to be former military.

Learning they were there to see her, Bess Monroe wrapped up her conversation and came toward them. She smiled tenderly at Max, who was wide awake, leaning happily against Garrett's wide chest, then turned back to Garrett and Hope with a frown. Directing them to an office with her name on the door, Bess shut the door behind them. Still holding Max, Garrett handled the introductions.

The registered nurse moved to the other side of her desk, but remained standing. "I told myself that if and when anyone from the Lockhart Foundation ever contacted me again, I would be cordial to them. No use burning any bridges when there is such desperate need, right? But…"

"I'm guessing your charity did not receive all of their funds, either," Hope prodded gently.

"Try any!" Bess exploded.

"None?" Garrett looked shocked.

Hope intervened. "The family really is trying to understand what's happened here, so they can make amends. It would be really helpful to us if you could share your experience."

Bess sat down and waited for them to take seats, too. "About a year ago, I drove to Dallas to meet with Lucille Lockhart at the foundation office. I explained the problem local veterans and their families were having, trying to get the support they needed, once they left active duty."

"Tank and Darcy Dunlop explained this to us."

Lucille nodded. "They're a great couple, and a perfect example. Although there are all kinds of problems that our nonprofit, West Texas Warrior Assistance, hopes to address."

"Like…?" Hope said, glad her hands were free so she could type notes into her phone.

"You want my wish list?"

Garrett nodded, holding a gurgling Max close.

"Temporary housing, close to the hospital. Support groups for warriors and every member of their family. Job counseling and placement. A separate rehab for those recovering from injuries incurred in battle, so they can still feel part of a team effort and urge each other on." Bess pulled a file out of her desk and handed it over. "A medical director familiar with combat injuries to coordinate care for the warriors and run the place. I could go on. And, in fact, I have. It's all in the pitch I gave your mother."

Trying not to notice how cute Max looked, snuggled

against Garrett's strong shoulder, Hope prompted, "So when you initially met with Lucille…?"

"She was really enthusiastic about our mission and she agreed to help us, with a one-time donation of a half a million dollars, to be paid out in monthly installments over the course of a year. All I had to do was formally demonstrate the need and present a business plan, which I did, and a letter of intent to donate would be forthcoming. Along with the first check to get us started."

Bess reached into her desk. "Here's the letter I received from the foundation, but there was no check with it. And, as you can see, the amount promised to us in writing was five thousand dollars, instead of five hundred thousand."

Hope expected Garrett to hand Max over to her. Instead, he shifted her son to one arm, held the document with the other. When he had finished perusing it, he provided it to Hope.

She, too, noted all was in order, then gave the letter back to Beth for safekeeping. "I assume you called the foundation to tell them of the error?"

Bess's expression was grim. "I was told by your mother's assistant, Sharla, that I would have to speak to Paul Smythe, the CFO about that. I did and he apologized profusely for the mistake, and promised that he would investigate and I would have a new letter of intent to donate and a check within the next few weeks."

Hope shared Garrett's obvious concern.

Bess threw up her hands in frustration. "I did not receive either one, and my subsequent calls went unreturned."

Noting Max appeared to be reaching for Hope, Garrett finally handed her son over. "When was the last time you contacted the foundation?" he asked in a low, rough tone that sent shivers of awareness sliding down Hope's spine.

"Several months ago. Anyway." Bess stood, signaling

their time had come to an end. "If you're worried I'm going to complain to the media, you needn't. I don't want what we're trying to do here to be any part of the bad publicity. I just want what was promised to us. That's all."

"WHY DIDN'T YOU reassure her you'd make things right?" Hope asked Garrett when they had left the hospital. She settled Max in his safety seat, then climbed into the passenger seat, once again letting Garrett drive since he knew the area better.

His broad shoulders flexed. He draped an arm along the back of the seat as he reversed the SUV out of the parking space. He paused to look her in the eye before shifting into drive. "Bess Monroe has suffered enough empty promises, don't you think?"

"You're on the board of directors, along with the rest of your family." Which meant he had sway.

"If someone has been stealing money from the foundation, there's no telling how much is actually left."

A breath-stealing notion. That the fifty-million-dollar Lockhart Foundation could be bankrupt was one she hadn't allowed herself to consider, until now. "So, what are you going to do?"

Garrett put the SUV in drive and turned out onto the street. "Wait for the results of the audit, look at everything, figure out where we stand. Then we'll make decisions on a priority basis."

"Kind of like a financial triage."

He nodded. "As far as right now…I need to drop by the real estate agency in town that is going to list my properties. The broker said it shouldn't take more than a couple of minutes to sign the papers." He gave her a second look. "If it's okay with you and Max. He's been a trouper so far."

"That he has. As opposed to last night…"

"I gather he doesn't normally wake up four times during a single night?"

So Garrett had noticed. "To nurse? No, he doesn't. But he was hungrier than usual last night."

In fact, they'd both been a little wound up.

Garrett shook his head fondly. "All that travelling."

"And being out on the ranch." She lifted a hand. "I'm kidding. He's a little young for any cowboy activity."

"I don't know." Garrett rubbed his jaw. "I could see him up on a horse someday."

So could she, oddly enough.

Garrett and herself, too.

Which was why she needed to put some barriers between them. Pronto.

"You're sure you don't want to come in with me?" Garrett asked, parking in front of the realtor's office.

"Actually, I'd like to stay out here and change Max's diaper."

He nodded. "I'll make it quick."

And he did. By the time she had finished, he was returning, folder full of papers in hand, a frown on his face.

She knew how it felt to face one difficulty after another. Despite her earlier resolve, her heart went out to him. "Problem?" she asked lightly, putting Max back into his car seat.

He climbed behind the wheel. "My tenants moved out a week ago and left the house in a mess, which wasn't a surprise, since they stiffed me on the final month's rent." He drew in an exasperated breath. "And there's a leak in the office building, which could mean substantial repairs before it can be put on the market."

Hope figured she owed him a favor, given how much help he had given her with Max. "You want to run by and quickly look in on both properties before we go back to the ranch?"

He exhaled in relief. "The office building first."

It was several blocks from the hospital, toward the edge of Laramie. Built of the terra-cotta brick popular many years past, it was three stories high and rectangular in shape. Inside, there were obvious leaks on the ceiling and one of the three elevators bore an Out of Order sign. All but two of the tenants had left, and they had signs up announcing their upcoming moves to other spaces.

Garrett grimaced. Hope could understand why. This was not going to be easy to sell, unless he wanted to severely undervalue it. She resisted the urge to reach out and squeeze his hand. "I'm guessing you had no idea it was this bad?"

Despite the tense circumstances, Garrett still managed to grin down at Max, who was trying to grab on to his shirt. "Let's put it this way. My dad always said the best deals were the opportunities no one else recognized or properly valued. And he was all about getting the best deal."

"Sounds like a hedge fund manager."

Garrett moved close enough to let Max latch on to his pinkie finger. He beamed proudly when Max met his goal.

Lucille's eldest son might not know it, Hope thought, a ribbon of warmth curling through her, but he had real daddy potential.

Oblivious to her admiring thoughts, Garrett continued, "My dad felt the same way about his personal life. He and my mom never bought a home they didn't plan on fixing up until it doubled in value."

Max rocked his tiny body toward their companion, as if signaling he wanted to be picked up. Garrett took her son in his arms. Watching, Hope's heart melted a little more.

Garrett shifted his palm a little higher, carefully supporting Max's back, shoulders and head. "My dad also felt people never really appreciated something unless they had to work for it."

"So the properties you and your siblings inherited…?" Hope asked, inhaling Garrett's brisk masculine scent as they walked through the building.

"All had good long-term value. And a heck of a lot of work to be done." He handed Max back to Hope, then paused to hold the door open.

"I'm guessing the house you were gifted is in the same shape as this office building."

"Let's put it this way. Just now, the listing agent said it had great potential."

"Code for fixer-upper?"

"Probably."

The heat of his smile made her tingle. "You haven't been there, either," she guessed.

Garrett fell into step beside them as they made their way to the parking area. "I've seen pictures. But at the time I inherited it, it was rented and I was stationed overseas, so… no. I haven't seen it." He touched her son's cheek. "Think the little guy can handle one more excursion?"

The question was, could *she* handle it? Already she felt a lot closer to Garrett. Not good when she was supposed to be keeping her distance. As their eyes met and held, Hope felt a shimmer of tension between them. Man–woman tension.

"We'd both love to see the second part of your inheritance," she murmured.

Located a half block away, the house was a large white Victorian with a wraparound porch. Inside it was, indeed, a mess. Trash in every room. Dust and cobwebs in every corner. Bathrooms that pretty much defied description. And yet…

Hope studied the original woodwork, high ceilings and

a plethora of windows in the century-old home. The house had multiple fireplaces. Gorgeous wood floors just begging to be refinished. A backyard made for entertaining.

Garrett turned to her, a peculiar look on his handsome face. "Like it...?"

Love it. Adore it. Hope shrugged, for all their sakes, pretending she wasn't head over heels in love with this property. Wasn't imagining herself and Max living in a place just like it someday. With a man just as kind and sexy and good-hearted, just as fundamentally decent as Garrett.

Realizing she was getting *way* ahead of herself, Hope forced her errant thoughts aside as they moved through the downstairs. It was post-pregnancy hormones. That was all.

She cleared her throat. "If you were to get a good cleaning crew in here..."

He stepped closer and her heart kicked into gear. "Or do it myself."

His pronouncement stopped her in her tracks. She did a double take. "*You'd* tackle this?" What was he, some sort of superhero Alpha Man?

The tiniest smile played around the corners of his chiseled lips. His gaze locked with hers. "I've tackled a lot of things in some of the places I've lived. I don't mind."

Something else to admire about him, Hope noted dreamily. The fact that he'd been born rich but could easily be comfortable in less luxurious circumstances.

She pushed the burgeoning attraction away.

She had to focus.

Had to remember he was the son of a client, nothing more. And speaking of the work she was supposed to be doing at this very second, she asked, "Are you going to have time to do that?"

"I've got another twenty-seven-and-a-half days of leave

left. So, yeah, I can and will do what is needed to get both properties on the market before I leave Texas."

And when that happened, when the crisis was over, her job finished, Garrett off to a job in either Seattle or DC, they'd likely never see each other again.

Nor would she have a reason to come back to the Circle H Ranch or Laramie County.

She had to remember that.

Stop fantasizing about what would never be.

She turned back to find Garrett studying her. "Problem?" he asked softly.

Not if I keep the proper perspective. Hope shook her head. "I'm just anxious to get back to the ranch. See how your mother and Adelaide are faring."

Chapter Five

Garrett walked into the Circle H bunkhouse, a wide-awake and slightly cranky Max snuggled in his big, strong arms. He took a moment to survey the scene. "Mom, you look like hell. You, too, Adelaide."

"Garrett!" Hope reprimanded him. She'd heard he was blunt, but wow! Although, she admitted reluctantly to herself, he was right.

In the three hours since she and Garrett had been gone, the long plank table had exploded with disorganized stacks of paperwork and multicolored file folders. Both women looked pale and completely overwhelmed. With his mother in her late sixties, and Adelaide's pregnancy, he was right to be concerned.

"When's the last time you-all ate?" he asked, reluctantly handing Max over to Hope.

The baby immediately began to fuss.

"I don't know." Adelaide and Lucille exchanged baffled looks. "Brunch, I guess, on the drive here."

"It's early, but you've got to have some dinner," Garrett decreed. "So we can either get back in the car and drive to town…"

All three women groaned at the thought of a twenty minute ride to Laramie and back. Never mind the time it might take to get seated, order and be served their meal. It would easily eat up a couple of hours.

Garrett headed for the kitchen. "Then I'm cooking."

If he cooked as well as he put together a sandwich, they were in luck. Eager to help, Hope said, "I need to feed Max and put him down. Then I'll give you a hand."

Garrett opened the fridge. "Take your time," he said over his shoulder. "I got this."

And he did, she found out some forty minutes later, when she emerged from the guest room where her son was fast asleep.

One end of the table had been cleared to allow for seats for four. Adelaide and Lucille had stopped working and were carrying table settings and the rest of the meal to the table.

Garrett was coming in through the mud-room door, a platter of burgers and roasted corn in hand. "I didn't know there was a grill out back," she said.

"A patio, glider and some outdoor rocking chairs, too," Lucille informed her. "I'm surprised you didn't notice that when you got here."

She might have, had it not been so late and she so enamored of her host's handsome son. If she hadn't taken time out to kiss him…

Guilt flooding through her, Hope shrugged.

Garrett's eyes crinkled at the corners, as if he, too, were recalling their steamy embrace and coveting another.

Wary of revealing herself, Hope quickly glanced away. Garrett gestured for everyone to have a seat. As they ate, he brought his mother up to date on their meeting with Bess Monroe.

"Sadly, her story matches the records I have," Lucille admitted unhappily.

"And those of many others," Adelaide concurred with

a worried frown. "Although we've yet to go through everything."

"What have you learned for sure?" Hope asked, wondering if there were any concrete facts she could work with to build a compelling narrative.

Hesitating, Adelaide looked over at Lucille, who nodded at her to continue. "A year ago, the foundation had fifty million in assets. Today, the foundation has only twenty-five million."

"Which is as it should be," Lucille said, "since we decided to give out twenty-five million in aid last year."

"So, where did the twenty-five million dollars go, if not all of it went to the earmarked charities?"

"We're still working on that."

"Meaning you think there is fraud involved." Garrett helped himself to a tangy vinegar-based coleslaw he'd found in the fridge.

"Certainly something untoward has gone on," the forensic accountant finally said.

"What, though, we don't yet know," Lucille said, cutting into a slice of watermelon. "The important thing is not to jump to any conclusions until we can show everything we have gathered to Paul."

The foundation CFO really needed to be there. *Now.* "When is he returning to Dallas?" Hope asked.

Adelaide exhaled. "My dad told me before he left he would be back home on Saturday afternoon, at two o'clock."

Or in roughly forty hours, Hope calculated, savoring the flavor of char-grilled beef and melted cheddar cheese nestled in a fresh brioche bun.

"We're planning to meet him at his home and bring him back to the ranch." Lucille looked pointedly at her son, clearly wanting a change of subject. "In the meantime, Sage called while you were out to check on things here and deliver her news."

"Something good, I gather?" Garrett added another burger to his plate.

Lucille beamed. "She's decided to move back to Texas as soon as she can arrange everything."

"Where in Texas?" Garrett asked.

"Here in Laramie, to her inheritance."

Garrett put down his fork. "Meaning…?"

"If the only reason you're considering moving to Seattle is to be close to your sister—don't."

Garrett sipped his iced tea. "Point taken, Mom."

An uncomfortable silence fell.

Hope wasn't sure what was going on. Was this Lucille lobbying for her son to move back to Texas? She'd told Hope she missed her children terribly. Wanted them all close to her again.

Enough to create a faux crisis with the foundation?

No, Hope immediately dismissed the notion. Whatever was going on here was real. And devastating. She had only to look at the shadows beneath Lucille's eyes to know that.

Garrett turned their conversation back to his little sister. "Does that mean Sage's finally given up on TW?"

Maybe it was the intimate setting, or the fact that Lucille had allowed Hope into her family's inner sanctum, at least long enough so that Hope could do her job, which compelled her to come right out and ask, "Who is TW?"

Adelaide sighed. "Terrence Whittier. This systems architect Sage has been following around for what…? Seven years now?"

Lucille nodded, clearly dismayed.

Garrett looked equally grim. "TW's made all sorts of promises to her, but kept none of them."

Lucille turned to her son. "I've taken a page from your

book, in this instance, and said it as bluntly as I can. Time is running out if Sage wants to meet someone else, get married and have a family."

Adelaide lifted a staying hand. "TW and Sage did break up two years ago, Lucille."

"But Sage didn't leave Seattle." Lucille fretted.

Garrett defended his sister. "She had just started her cowgirl chef business up there, Mom. It was going great."

Hope could understand not wanting to leave that.

Lucille worried the strand of pearls around her neck. "I have a feeling TW came back in her life last winter— at least briefly."

Garrett assumed his usual poker face. "Did she tell you that?"

"No." Lucille looked at her eldest son steadily. "She didn't have to tell me. I'm a mother. I just know these things."

"Is that the way it is?" Garrett asked Hope later, when they were alone once again. His mother and Adelaide had gone to bed, vowing to get up early and pick up where they had left off.

He followed her into the mud room, where the washer and dryer were located. Hope wished she could say she was immune to his charm; she wasn't. There was just something really satisfying about spending time with him, even when they were doing really mundane things like errands, or dishes or, best of all, baby care. "Do mothers just instinctively know things about their kids?" he continued.

Hope sorted baby clothes and blankets into whites and pastel blues and dropped the latter into the tub. Eager to get the spit-up laundered out of all their garments, she added her own similarly hued shirts and pajamas. "Sort of. At least, I do."

She turned toward him. Inhaling his brisk masculine

scent and the mint on his breath, it was all she could do not to think about kissing him again. "I read up a lot on infants and the ways they communicate before Max was born. For instance, when he's hungry, he makes a *meh* sound. It's supposed to be *neh*, but I think he's combining that with Mommy, and it comes out *meh*."

Garrett grinned at her maternal bragging, as she meant him to.

Proudly, Hope continued, "When Max is sleepy he yawns. And when he has air in the tummy he wants to get out, he makes an *eh* or *earh* sound."

Garrett rummaged around the cabinet until he produced a bottle of extra-gentle laundry detergent. "When he needs a diaper change?"

The backs of their fingers brushed as he gave the detergent to her. Ignoring the resultant tingle, Hope concentrated on measuring the clear liquid into the cap, then pouring it into the dispenser. "He kicks his legs a lot and says *huh* repeatedly."

Garrett shifted, his big body exuding warmth in the small space. "Does he get mad at you?"

"Sometimes." Hope set the dials, switched on the washer, then left the room before being with him in the small space revved up her latent desire and them falling into each other's arms again. "Like when we're driving somewhere and I can't stop until we get there. Although," she added, continuing into the kitchen to help herself to one last glass of milk before bed, "if Max has to wait more than five minutes for me to be able to stop and get him out of his car seat, the motion of the vehicle usually lulls him to sleep."

Garrett surprised her by pouring himself a glass of milk, too. "So, even when you do have to drive a little longer than Max would like, it's not so bad." He stepped into the pantry, emerging with a bag of gourmet butter cookies.

Hope accepted one. "For either of us." Keeping her voice low, so as not to wake anyone, she stepped out onto the front porch of the bunkhouse. There, she could hear Max if he cried.

The night was warm and breezy, the velvety black Texas sky was sprinkled with stars surrounding a brilliant yellow quarter moon.

Leaning against a porch post, she looked over at Garrett, who seemed to be enjoying the late summer evening on the ranch as much as she was.

His gaze roved the messy confines of the knot on the top of her head. "Have you heard from your nanny?"

Aware she hadn't done a very good job of putting her hair up in an elastic band before she'd nursed Max the last time, Hope set her glass on the rail. Determined to appear at least a little more professional, and less Mommy On Vacation, she reached up and shook her hair out, combing it with her fingers as best she could.

"Mary Whiting? Yes. She emailed me this afternoon. Her mom's heart surgery was successful,"

Which was really great—for Mary and her family.

"But it's going to be at least a six- to eight-week recuperation. And Mary is going to stay with her family to help out."

Which was really bad—for her and Max.

"Can you get another nanny?"

"The agency is already sending me candidate profiles for an interim replacement."

He came near enough she could feel his body heat. "But…?"

Ignoring the melting sensation in her tummy, Hope lifted a shoulder. "Mary's going to be hard to replace, even temporarily. She was perfect with Max. He hasn't bonded with anyone so readily except yo—uh…er…"

Oh, darn, had she really almost said that?

Apparently, judging by the supreme masculine satisfaction emanating from him, she had.

DELIGHTEDLY TRACKING THE flush that started in her chest and crept up to her face, Garrett palmed the center of his chest. "Me?"

She thought about trying to deny it but realized that was pointless. "Surely you noticed how much Max loves it when you hold him…"

Garrett shrugged. "I love holding him, too."

That said, he gazed at her lips. Her breath caught as he took her glass. Set it aside. Bent his head.

The next thing Hope knew she was all the way against him. His arms were wrapped around her. Their mouths were fused.

If anything, this kiss was sweeter than the first they had shared.

Shorter, too.

He drew back. Enough light poured out from the interior of the house that she could see the desire glimmering in his eyes.

She had sure as heck *felt* it in his kiss.

Her chest rose and fell as she tried to find the will to admonish him, but the words just wouldn't come. So she did the only thing she could. She picked up her glass and disappeared into the house and then her bedroom, shutting the door firmly behind her.

Garrett knew he was pushing the boundaries Hope had set. But with only a few days to convince her they had something worth pursuing, he had kissed her, anyway.

Felt her respond.

And knew all he had to do was continue getting to know

her—and her adorable little son—and let the rest of the situation play out. Go from there.

In the meantime, they all needed sleep, so he headed to bed.

He was awakened at one thirty in the morning, when Max cried.

"Meh...meh...meh..."

Which meant, Garrett knew now, Max was hungry.

The house fell silent once again.

Which meant Hope was nursing.

Two hours later, Max woke again, demanding to be fed. Eventually the house grew quiet.

At five thirty, Max woke for the third time in six hours. "Meh...meh...meh..." And this time, he wouldn't stop.

Garrett lay in bed, wondering if he should offer to help, or stay put and let Hope deal with it as expertly as she usually did.

The sound of the front door opening and a crying Max being carried outside had him vaulting out of bed.

He joined Hope and the baby in the yard.

She was standing with her hand on the car door, tears streaming down her face. And still an apparently hungry—and healthy—Max cried. "Meh, meh, meh."

"What's going on?" Garrett asked, gathering the infant into his arms.

Hope was still in her menswear-style pajamas, which were buttoned crookedly up the front, her hair a tousled mess. She had her keys but no purse.

And the tears continued to spill from her eyes. "Max wants to nurse again," she sobbed softly, "and my breasts are dry!"

He could see where that was a problem, a big one, for both mother and child. Resisting the urge to take Hope in his arms, along with Max, and hold them both close, he asked, "So what's the plan?" Obviously, she had one.

Hope let out a shuddering breath and ran both her hands through her hair. Her chest rose and fell with each agitated breath. "To drive him back and forth on the ranch until he falls asleep again. Or I make more milk." She gestured helplessly. "Whichever comes first."

The physician in him rose to the challenge. He met and held her eyes. "I have a better plan. Why don't you go inside and get dressed?"

Chapter Six

Ten minutes later, a fully dressed Hope climbed into the back of the SUV next to her intermittently wailing son. Garrett slipped his phone into the pocket of his shirt and settled behind the wheel. From the doorway, Lucille and Adelaide, who had been awakened by all the ruckus, waved.

Embarrassed that she was turning out to be so inept a mother, at a time when she most needed to be at her best, Hope drew a deep breath.

She knew she shouldn't need a man in her life. And she didn't. But it was sure nice to have Garrett here right now. Even better that he was a doctor.

"You're sure we should take Max to the emergency room?" she asked, as he started the drive to town. She couldn't help but worry that she was overreacting, as she had a tendency to do when it came to her twelve-week-old son.

Yet Max's continued distress, his persistent crying, his absolute refusal to take his pacifier was real. As was the lack of milk in her breasts, the soreness of her tender nipples. Although none of that was a surprise, given how often he had been nursing in the last thirty-six hours.

Garrett nodded confidently.

He had taken the time to brush his teeth and splash some water on his face, as had she. He hadn't shaved, and the rim of beard on his face gave him a ruggedly handsome look.

"Lacey McCabe is the best pediatrician in the area. She agreed to meet us there, before her rounds. Make sure there's nothing wrong."

"But you're a physician. Can't you tell?" *Put my mind at ease right now!*

He cast her a brief, consoling look in the rearview mirror. "I'm an internist who specializes in traumatic injuries—and recovery—in soldiers. Max needs a pediatrician, and although it might be able to be handled over the phone, Lacey and I both agreed it would be better if he was seen."

Hope couldn't argue with that.

Plus, she appreciated Garrett's protectiveness toward her son, which mirrored her own.

"Besides," he continued in a raspy growl. Finding the aviator sunglasses he'd hooked in the opening of his shirt, he slipped them on, obscuring his gorgeous blue eyes from view. "I'm emotionally involved."

Just that suddenly, something came and went in the air between them. The slightest spark of hope of all-out romance.

Hope gave Max's pacifier yet another try. To her relief, this time her son accepted it and began to suckle, his little lips working furiously.

Needing to understand exactly what Garrett meant by "emotionally involved," and appreciating the blissful silence that fell in the interior of her SUV, Hope asked, "You mean with Max?"

Garrett's hands tightened on the steering wheel. His voice dropped another notch. "With both of you." Oblivious to the leaping of her heart, he kept his attention on the road. "A smart doctor never treats those he is close to—it's too easy to let your feelings get in the way and overlook something you don't want to see."

Like what? Hope wondered, feeling the weight of his concern.

"Then this could be serious?" she probed nervously, as Max abruptly spit out his pacifier and continued his *meh meh meh*...albeit a little more softly and a lot more hoarsely.

She saw Garrett's lips tighten in the rearview mirror, but when he spoke it was with a physician's calm. "Yes, but there's a much higher chance it's not. Still, with a child this young, it's just best not to take any chances."

Hope nodded and turned her attention back to her son, doing everything she could think to soothe him, but nothing worked. Not the touch of her hands, the motion of the vehicle or her voice. Not even the relaxing music when Garrett turned on the stereo. Max fussed the entire way, his hoarse cries breaking her heart—to the point that she was wiping away tears herself.

Finally, they pulled into the emergency entrance of the Laramie Community Hospital and parked in a slot designated for ER patients. Her breasts aching—and empty— Hope struggled to pull it together. She was not going to let Max down even more. She was *not* going to cry.

"We'll get this taken care of in no time. Just hang in there," Garrett said, his voice a tender caress.

He leaped out to assist.

Unfortunately, by the time Hope got Max out of his car seat he was in full temper, arching his back and wailing at the top of his lungs. Hoping Garrett could calm him, Hope handed her son over, then emerged from the car herself.

To her chagrin, Max didn't appear to want either of them to hold him. So Hope settled him back in her arms. Worse, his wails sounded all the louder in the early morning quiet of the emergency room.

Luckily, they had staff waiting for them.

To her surprise, the nurse approaching them looked familiar, except her hair was different. Longer.

"I'm Bess Monroe's twin, Bridgett Monroe," the woman said, apparently used to the confusion. She grabbed a clipboard and pen as they passed the admitting desk. "We're both nurses here. I usually work in the hospital nursery, but Dr. McCabe asked me to come down for this. So…" Bridgett smiled, assessing their trio. "You're Hope Winslow and this indignant little fella is Max?"

"Right."

Bridgett turned to their gallant escort. "And you're the Dr. Garrett Lockhart I spoke with on the phone?"

Garrett nodded his greeting, abruptly looking all confident, capable military physician. "Affirmative."

"Nice to meet you, Doc. Did you want to come back to the exam area or stake out a place in the waiting room?"

It took Hope no time at all to decide the answer to that. "I'd like him with us." She paused, wondering belatedly if she had overstepped, and searched his eyes. "Is that okay?"

Looking as though there was no place else he would rather be, Garrett volunteered, "I can hold him while you fill out the paperwork."

Together they went into the exam room. While Hope answered the questions on the hospital intake forms, Garrett propped Max up on his shoulder and walked him back and forth, whispering soft, soothing words in his ear all the while.

Max rested his head on Garrett's big shoulder, his fussing finally beginning to lessen. Seconds later, Dr. Lacey McCabe walked in. The petite, silvery blond pediatrician introduced herself, then asked Garrett to put Max on the exam table. Bridgett stepped in to help undress the infant and assisted with the physical exam. When she had finished, Lacey swaddled Max in an ER blanket and handed him to Hope for comforting. Stethoscope still wrapped around her neck, Lacey pulled up a stool and indicated for them to get comfortable, too. "Tell me what's going on."

Hope settled on the gurney, Max in her arms. Garrett stood close beside her while she brought the pediatrician up to date.

Lacey listened while the nurse typed into a computer tablet. "And up to now you've been feeding on demand?"

"Yes." Hope was glad Max had quieted, at least temporarily, now that he was back in her arms, his pacifier in his mouth.

"And that's worked well for you?" Dr. McCabe continued. "His weight gain has been on track?"

About that, Hope could brag. "It's been perfect."

"But otherwise, you've been able to keep up your milk supply?"

Hope felt a surge of regret. "Until I went back to work earlier this week."

"How has that been going?" the doctor asked empathetically.

Not nearly as great as I'd like it to be.

Garrett reached over and squeezed her shoulder. Appreciating his support, Hope leaned into his touch while she answered the pediatrician's questions. "It's complicated," she said finally.

Understanding shone in Lacey's gaze. "Stressful?"

"Um, yes…and no. It just sort of depends on what is going on, like in all jobs."

"But the last few days in particular…?" Dr. McCabe prodded.

The heat of embarrassment welled in Hope's chest. "Have been pretty stressful," she admitted reluctantly. "What with Max's nanny getting called away on a family emergency, just when we needed her most." If it hadn't been for Garrett during the last couple of days, she honestly didn't know how they would have coped.

Lacey nodded. "Okay. Well, there's a good reason why you and Max are out of sync. And, just so you know, it happens to all new moms when they make the transition from maternity leave to work. It does get better."

"Thank heaven." Hope sighed, suddenly feeling on the verge of tears again. "Because I'm not sure I could take it if Max continued to want to nurse every two hours instead of every three or four!"

"Unfortunately, that may not happen for a while," Lacey warned her. "Max is in a growth spurt. And like all healthy males, he wants what he wants when he wants it."

Everyone in the room chuckled at the pediatrician's joke, including Garrett.

Hope met his eyes.

He shook his head, grinning.

A new spiral of warmth slid through her.

Humor, she realized, could do a lot to get them through. Well, that and a little romance…

"So, there are two options," Dr. McCabe continued, bringing Hope back to the problem at hand. "One, is to tough it out and let your innate maternal response to your baby's distress push your body into producing more milk. That usually takes a few days. The other is to keep nursing at a rate you feel comfortable with and supplement with formula to give your body a little break," Lacey continued with a nonjudgmental practicality and compassion Hope really appreciated. "Which is what I did when my six daughters were young. I found combination feeding was the best of both worlds for me."

Lacey paused to let Hope consider.

"But it's really up to you, Hope. Both options are perfectly fine. It just depends on what you, as Max's mother, want to do."

That was easy, Hope thought in relief. "I'd like to try the combination."

Lacey McCabe stood. "Okay, then how about we set you up with a day's supply of formula until you can get to the pharmacy or grocery on your own. And in the meantime, Hope?" The pediatrician paused at the exam room door. "Be sure you drink enough fluids, take in enough calories and get plenty of rest. You need to take care of yourself, too."

"I second that," Garrett said, as soon as the nurse and doctor had exited. He stroked Max's head, paused to look deeply into Hope's eyes, demonstrating once again what a good father—and husband—he would make someday.

A thread of wistfulness swept through her.

"And to that end," he added gruffly, as her gratitude grew by leaps and bounds, "I'll do whatever I can to assist you both."

Short minutes later, Hope watched Max finish the bottle in no time flat.

"And here I thought he might not like the taste of formula," she murmured, turning her son upright to give him one last burp.

Garrett, who had been texting his mom to let her know that Max was okay, put his cell phone back in his pocket. He shook his head fondly at both of them. "You know how it is when you're really hungry…"

She warmed at his lazy once-over. However, just because he was being exceptionally kind and considerate did not mean he was auditioning to be the man in her life. "Good point." Flushing slightly, she put Max down and, while changing his diaper, drew a stabilizing breath and worked to keep up the witty repartee. "When you're famished, anything tastes good." And some things, like Garrett's kiss, were amazingly good...

She had to stop thinking this way.

Letting her fatigue, and her current need to lean on someone's strong shoulder, make more of their temporary friendship than there was.

Garrett picked up the diaper bag and her purse. Some men would have looked ridiculous carrying both. The contrast only made him look more impossibly masculine. Sea-blue eyes twinkling, he held the door for her and Max. "Well, there are some things I don't think I'd like, regardless."

Hope wondered how much she had really put him out the last few days. Garrett acted as if charging to her rescue—continually—was nothing. She knew better. He had important decisions to make. And only so much military leave. There were also family and friends he probably wanted to spend more time with. Yet he'd remained with her and Max, even though his brother Chance had dropped a Bull Haven Ranch pickup off for him the previous morning.

"In fact, there are some things I downright loathe." He chuckled.

Hope fell into step beside him. "Like...?"

He escorted her outside. The air was warm and scented with flowers, the sky a clear light blue overhead.

"Pickled beets. Can't stand 'em."

Hope couldn't help but laugh. "Me, either," she murmured, as a yawning Max drowsily watched them both.

Garrett shortened his steps as they wound their way through the parked vehicles in the emergency services lot. When they reached the car, he leaned in to help Hope get a now-asleep Max into his safety seat.

"Well, what do you know?" Garrett observed with a

tenderness that nearly stopped Hope's breath. "He's fast asleep."

Hope luxuriated in the shared emotion. It was at times like this that she missed having a daddy for Max, and a husband for herself, the most.

"No wonder." Deliberately, she returned her attention to her son. He looked as precious as could be, his long blond lashes resting against his cheeks, his bow-shaped lips working soundlessly. "He wore himself out…"

Whereas she—and Garrett—both seemed to be running on adrenaline.

Because it would be easier to talk quietly if she were seated beside Garrett, Hope climbed into the front seat of her SUV. Once again aware of how cozy and domestic this all felt, she asked, "What did your mom have to say when you texted?"

He squared his jaw and kept his eyes on the road. "She and Adelaide are glad Max is okay."

Uh-huh. And what else? Feminine instinct told her that he was deliberately holding something back. "And…?"

He hit the signal and turned left, which was, if memory served, not the way out of town toward the Circle H.

"They need more information from the bank if they're going to figure out where all the money went. The only way to quickly take a look at the cancelled checks, and discover where they were being deposited, is to go to the foundation's bank in person. So they're driving back this morning. They left as soon as they knew Max was okay."

Or in other words, twenty minutes ago.

Hope settled back in her seat, not sure how she felt about that. She turned to study Garrett's handsome profile. "When will they return?"

"Tomorrow, at the earliest. Depends on how quickly they're able to get all the data."

Aware she hadn't checked any of her work messages since close of business the previous day—a definite mistake when in the midst of any scandal—Hope pulled out her cell phone. In work mode once again, she bit her lip. "I wonder if we should go back to Dallas, too."

"I texted that option while you were feeding Max, back at the hospital. Mom said she would prefer we sit tight. She will call us as soon as they discover anything. But right now her plan is to return to the ranch with Adelaide, and Paul, as soon as possible. And go from there."

Nodding, Hope scanned the Dallas news headlines on the internet.

Garrett slanted her a glance. "Anything?"

"Six more charities have come forward to say they were stiffed by the foundation. But it's only a mention." Hope sighed her relief that the ugly gossip was dying down. "Not the lead story."

"Is that good?"

"It means public interest is waning—for now. It'll crank back up again as soon as we learn whether the foundation is at fault or not and people begin to react to that."

Sighing, she put her phone back in her purse.

"You need to eat something." Garrett detoured into a drive-through restaurant famous for its breakfast tacos.

He ordered two for her, three for himself, a couple of hash brown potato patties, coffee and milk.

He handed her the bag, then headed back out on the road.

They ate in the car, knowing that if they stopped for long Max would likely wake. Happily, Max slept for the rest of the ride back to the ranch.

Together they eased him out of the car, into the bunkhouse and into his bed. Realizing how lucky they were that Garrett had been there to help them, and Max's health crisis had been so easily resolved, Hope stood a moment, just drinking in the sight of her baby boy, memorizing everything about him. With his cheeks full of healthy color, one tiny fist tucked under his chin as he slept, he looked so sweet and peaceful. Emotion clogged her throat.

She turned away and walked out of the room.

Garrett followed her, his steps as silent and languid as his mood.

Suddenly feeling unutterably fragile, Hope kept her back to him and said what she should have a lot earlier, "I owe you a lot for this morning. In fact, for the entire past few days…"

She wouldn't have been able to get any work done without him. Max was certainly better off, too, with Garrett there.

He put a light hand on her shoulder. "Glad to help," he told her huskily, turning her around.

The next thing she knew, instinct was taking over. She was all the way against him, wrapped in his strong, steady warmth. His head slanted, dipped. And then there was no stopping it. Everything she felt, everything she wanted, was right there, in that moment, in his arms.

GARRETT HAD PROMISED himself he wouldn't kiss Hope again or let things get out of hand. At least, not until the foundation scandal was over and he could pursue her the way he wanted to pursue her—with no holds barred.

But the moment she turned her vulnerable green eyes to his and launched herself against him, all previous resolutions were off. She made a sexy little sound in the back of her throat as her mouth softened under his, opening to allow him deeper access.

"What are you doing to me?" she whispered. "What are we doing to each other…?" And then her hands were coming up to cup his head. She was standing on tiptoe, pressing her body against him, tangling her tongue with his.

Had she not surrendered so completely to the pressure of his mouth against hers, maybe it would have been a lot easier to do the gallant thing and walk away. Before things heated up even more.

But she didn't pull away. Nor did he.

He felt the need pouring out of her, matching his own. Felt the barriers around her heart lower, just a little bit. Because Hope was right about one thing—whatever he was doing to her, she was doing it to him, too.

Succumbing to the moment, he pulled her in a little closer, a little tighter, enjoying the heady rush of their adrenaline-fueled tryst, and she was right there with him, surrendering, even as she demanded more.

He had an idea she'd regret this.

But for now, she was all about the moment.

And he knew this wasn't an experience likely to come again. At least, not any time soon. So he went with it, lifting her so her legs wrapped around his waist and carrying her, still kissing, all the way to his bed.

They tumbled down onto it. She shoved him to his back and sprawled on top of him.

He groaned softly, thinking that he deserved a swift kick in the rear for doing this. There wasn't a smidgen of commitment between them and Hope wasn't anywhere near a one-night-stand woman.

Still struggling with his conscience, Garrett lifted his head long enough to rasp, "I feel like I'm taking advantage."

"Don't," she whispered back, kissing his jaw, his cheek, his lips with wild abandon. "I'm a grown woman. I know exactly what I'm doing."

Did she?

He wondered. Yet, when she spread her hands across

his chest and shoulders, caressing, molding, exploring, he couldn't help but haul her even closer and kiss her again.

"And I'm pretty sure..." she murmured, letting her quest drift lower to the proof of his desire "...the one taking advantage here..." she sighed with obvious delight as his body went hard and he swore, low and rough "...would be me."

His hands tightened on her, squeezed. She smelled so good, tasted so good, felt so good. "You're certain this is what you want?" he gritted out.

She looked him in the eye, confirming lustily, "What I need."

Well, what do you know? You're what I need right now, too. "Okay, then," he said with a reckless grin that matched her own. "Permission granted."

Emerald eyes sparkling, she unbuttoned his shirt, spread the edges wide. Admired, even as she kissed his shoulders and chest. Sensually explored her way down the goody trail to the clasp of his belt. Kissed her way back up even more slowly and decadently.

"Not to worry." She paused to make a thorough tour of his mouth. "We'll apologize and forgive each other later," she promised, her honey-blond hair sliding across his skin.

No, he thought, we won't.

He wasn't surprised she had already anticipated her next move, though.

This was the Hope he'd first met. Dynamic. Determined to be in charge. Following a plan and focused on a goal. Which, at the moment, was making love with him while irrefutably dismissing the possibility of anything more.

Figuring they could sort all that out later, after they'd rocked each other's worlds, he ran a hand up the inside of her thigh. She shot to her knees, her smooth, velvety skin quivering and warming beneath his palm. Lips parted, breath erratic, she rose above him and splayed her hands across his chest, seeming to dare him to make her want him even half as much as he already yearned for her.

Little did she know how up to the task he was. Libido roaring, he shifted her so she was beneath him. He unwrapped her with delight—first her shorts and panties, then her blouse and bra.

She was even more beautiful than he had imagined. With soft, full breasts, a slender waist, rounded tummy and sleek, gorgeous thighs.

Clearly appreciating his admiration, nipples tightening into hard buds of arousal, she unfastened his belt. "Let's see what you've got, Captain."

"Yes, ma'am." He rose long enough to strip down, too.

Her eyes moved over him, in sweet, solemn awe that sent his pulse roaring even more.

"That," he told her, moving back over top of her, pressing the hard ridge of his erection against her welcoming softness, "is what you do to me."

She drew in a halting breath, said, "Then let's see what *you* can do to *me*."

Chapter Seven

It was a challenge, Hope soon realized, Garrett was completely up for. He caught her against him, so they were flush against each other, tunneled his hands through her hair and fitted his mouth to hers, giving her a long, thorough kiss designed to shatter her resolve. Until she was no longer able or willing to put any limits whatsoever on their lovemaking.

Excitement flooded through her. She sank into him, luxuriating in the hard length of him and the overwhelming provocativeness of his kiss.

"Oh, my…" she whispered long minutes later, when he finally lifted his head. When had simply making out—naked—been this incredible? When had any man been this sexy and tender and kind? Or left her feeling so completely wanton and desirable?

"My feelings exactly," Garrett rasped. Gazing into her eyes, he cupped the side of her face with his large hand. Kissed her again—hotly, possessively—then slid down her body, stopping to caress and kiss every inch along the way—the curves of her breasts, the sensitive tips, the dip of her waist, the belly still rounded from childbirth. Lower still, to the nest of soft curls and the blossoming dampness within.

The pressure of his mouth, coupled with the questing

caress of his fingertips, sent her arching up off the bed. The rough wild rasp of his tongue, coupled with his gentle suckling, catapulted her all the way over the edge. Her cry of ecstasy had him chuckling in masculine satisfaction. His heart pounding in tandem to her own, he moved up her body. Found the condom in his wallet, and swiftly rolled it on.

Ready to see to his own needs, he eased between her thighs, taking her in one smooth, deep stroke. The rhythmic pressure of his body and his mouth took her to new heights, making her burn and tingle and *want* inside. She teetered on the edge of something thrilling and wonderful, yearning for more than she had ever thought possible, as he transported her to a place where she had never been. A place that was not just sexy as all get-out, but safe and warm and oh-so immensely satisfying, too.

It was just too bad, she thought dazedly, as they slowly stopped shuddering and returned to reality, it could never happen again.

GARRETT FELT THE change in Hope as soon as their breathing returned to normal. Reluctantly he disengaged their bodies and shifted his weight to the side, but did not let her go. Although this was what he had expected all along— a ready ticket to the exit—he could not say he welcomed it. He knew their situation was complicated. Complicated was more than okay when it led to results like this. He just had to convince her of that.

"Regrets?" He kissed her temple.

Still trembling, Hope closed her eyes and didn't answer, preventing him once again from getting lost in her emerald-green eyes.

Determined to ease her worries, he smoothed a hand through her silky mane. "If you're worried about a conflict of interest—don't be. I wouldn't have hired you. I still wouldn't hire you." He chuckled. "Or any scandal manager for that matter."

She met his gaze. Her eyes were filled with mischief. "That's good to know. I wouldn't have accepted a job working for you, either."

That he could believe. He bent to kiss the inside of her wrist. Her elbow. Shoulder. "Then?"

Hope rose and, sheet draped around her, perched wearily on the edge of the bed. She grabbed her clothes off the floor. Keeping her back to him, she slipped on her bra, fastened it in front. "When people see a resolution to a crisis, they feel exultant and relieved, reckless and needy."

He lay back on his side, watching as she slipped her arms into the sleeves of her blouse. Although the sheet obscured the lower half of her, he could well remember the lissome lines of her hips and thighs, the sweet spot in between.

He felt himself grow hard again.

"This has happened to you before, then?"

Her eyes drifted lower and she caught her breath. Discreetly eased her way into her panties. Stood. "No. I've never been involved with a client." She stepped into her shorts, apparently oblivious to the fact that he found it just as arousing to watch her get dressed as it had been to undress her, just minutes earlier.

She wound her hair into a knot at the base of her neck and secured it there with one of the elastic bands she always seemed to have wrapped around her wrist whenever she was caring for Max.

Walking into his bathroom, she bent and splashed some cold water onto her face, pausing to dry her face and look into the mirror.

From his vantage point on the bed, he saw her stare at

her flushed cheeks and passion-glazed eyes, as if seeing a stranger. Her breasts rose as she took a deep enervating breath. Then turned, all cool reserve once again, and walked back into the bedroom to join him.

She bent and tossed him his clothes. "I'm always orchestrating the end of a crisis. I'm not involved in it." She turned her back, wanting to continue this conversation. But clearly, he realized, not so long as he was hard and naked.

Reluctantly, he shucked on his boxers and jeans.

The erection he could do nothing about.

When she heard the rasp of his zipper, she turned back to him. Face pale, she said, upset all over again, "But this morning, with Max suddenly in such distress—the fact we had to take him to the ER—made me realize all over again how much I love him and want to protect him." Her eyes grew misty, her voice turned hoarse. "The idea that there might come a time I might not be able to keep him safe and healthy, really rocked me to the core."

He nodded, understanding.

What would any of them do without Max?

Without any of the people they loved in their lives?

He'd felt the same jolt of fear and anxiety when his father had been diagnosed with a degenerative heart disease.

Yet loss, in every life, was inevitable.

Which was where faith came in. Faith and the people around you…

"Which is why you turned to me," he guessed, pulling on his shirt.

Hope wiped away her tears before they fell. She squared her shoulders, and seemed to pull herself together, as she surveyed his chest. "Well, that and your hot bod," she teased.

He winked, following her easy lead. "Turned you on, did I?"

"I admit it. You're so different from the men I usually

date. I was curious what it would be like to hit the sheets with you."

He came closer, aware he didn't like the mental image of her in any other guy's arms. "What kind of men do you usually go out with?" he asked gruffly, already wondering how to get rid of the competition.

She tapped her index finger on her chin. "Tactful."

Ha-ha. "You mean wusses?"

She shook her head. "Nonmilitary."

"So in other words, execs…"

"One reporter."

"Your basic white-collar types."

"Yes."

The kind of guy, he figured, she could probably dominate. The kind of guy that, in the end, would bore her silly. He tilted his head and flashed her a cocky grin. "You've been missing out."

For a moment, she seemed to agree. At least in bed. Which made him wonder. "So, now that your curiosity about my sexual prowess has been satisfied…?" He fished around for a little more information.

"I realize you are talented in many areas."

He laughed, as she'd meant him to.

The impishness in her gaze faded. She touched his wrist in a way that felt like goodbye. Slowly met his eyes. "Seriously. I'm sorry if I took advantage of you."

He shrugged and caught her hand with his. "I think it was mutual."

She disengaged their palms, stepped back, all professional scandal manager. "In any case, it won't happen again."

His gaze drifted over her lazily. "You really don't think so?" Because if it were up to him, it would.

Her conflicted attitude faded as fast as it had appeared. She walked out into the kitchen, poured herself a glass of milk. "I get that we had fun here, Garrett. But I have a job to do. That has to take precedence."

He helped himself to a bottle of water, took a long thirsty drink, before promising, "I won't interfere with that."

He could see she didn't believe him. But she had stopped trying to run away. Garrett decided to try another tack. He leaned back against the counter. "Did you ever see *When Harry Met Sally*?"

Hope stopped in mid-sip. "One of the greatest romantic comedies of all time? Ah, yeah, about a million times when I was growing up." She lounged opposite him, a curious expression on her face.

"Well, so did Sage."

Understanding dawned. "Which meant you watched it a lot, too."

Way too many times. Or so he'd thought then. Later, he had realized what valuable information the movie contained about the differences between the sexes when it came to dating and relationships.

"You know those little vignettes that were woven throughout, about how couples met each other?" he continued.

"And fell in love?" Finishing her milk, she sighed in wistful appreciation. "They were all so funny and unique. And real."

And she deserved even more than that. "Well, this is our story, Hope." He took her glass, put it aside and drew her back into his arms. "And one day soon, maybe even today, you'll look back and see our initial hookup was even more original than any of those."

She splayed her hands across his chest. "You're sure that's all this is? A hookup?"

He rubbed the pad of his thumb across the softness of her cheek. "Would it make you feel better if it were?"

She hesitated, but just for a millisecond. "Between work and Max, it's really all I have room for in my life right now."

He could understand that. What she didn't know was that she wouldn't be this busy—or conflicted—forever. He lowered his mouth to hers, fibbed, "Then that's what it is."

And before she could argue further, he made love to her again.

HOPE NEVER MEANT to fall asleep. She meant to get up out of the bed after they'd made sweet, wonderful love the second time. But the next thing she knew late afternoon sunlight was streaming in through the windows and she heard her son gurgling happily.

She glanced at her watch. Realizing it had been a good seven hours since she had fed Max last, she threw back the covers, wrapped a sheet around herself and headed for her bedroom.

The port-a-crib was empty.

The laughter, however, continued. This time with Garrett joining in.

Hope exchanged the sheet for her robe and followed the sound.

Garrett was slouched on the big U-shaped bunkhouse sofa, his back to her, Max held upright against his chest. Plump little arms out in front of him, as if he were doing push-ups, Max was staring up at Garrett, enthralled.

"See here's the thing about women," Garrett was telling Max. "You always got to treat 'em right. I know, I know," he replied, after another spurt of baby talk from Max, "you think you're too young to be thinking about all this, but trust me, there will come a day, and that's all you'll be thinking about…"

Max gurgled again, then let out an astonishingly loud burp.

Hope couldn't help it, she laughed, right along with Garrett.

He turned in surprise. "Did we wake you?"

"I think the bigger question is," she murmured, joining him on the sofa, "why didn't you get me?" She nodded at the empty bottle of formula on the coffee table. "I would have fed him."

"I know. I thought it might be better for you to get some sleep."

Garrett was probably right, given the fact that her breasts still only felt half full. It would be at least another hour, if not more, before she was ready to nurse her son again.

She kissed the tuft of blond hair on the top of Max's head. Though normally he reached for Hope, insisting that his mommy hold him, this time her son seemed remarkably content just where he was. "How long has he been up?"

Garrett grinned as Max continued to do vertical baby push-ups against his chest. "A couple of hours."

Hope did a double take.

Garrett slanted her a glance. "He hasn't seemed to want to go back to sleep."

She wouldn't either, if Garrett were holding her like that in his big, strong arms and turning on the charm.

Hope snuggled closer, wanting to join in the fun. "What have you two been doing?"

"Well, first he had a bottle of formula, then a clean diaper change, then we went out back and sat on the glider for a while. But it got kind of hot, so we came in to the air conditioning. And we lay on a blanket on the floor for a while, and he showed me all his toys and rattles. And then we sat in a chair...and then you came in..."

"Wow."

"I know," Garrett acknowledged solemnly. "Max and I have had a very busy afternoon."

She peered at him facetiously. "You sure you don't want a job filling in for a British nanny on an emergency basis?"

Rubbing a hand across his freshly shaven jaw, he pretended to consider it. Finally he asked, with a teasing leer, "Does it come with fringe benefits?"

Hope groaned facetiously. She slapped a hand across her heart as if the mere idea were an insult. "Captain Lockhart!"

"Uh-oh, buddy." Garrett winked at Max. "She's using my rank and surname. Guess we better rein in the loose talk."

No kidding, Hope thought. Otherwise he'd have her back in bed with him before she knew what had happened.

Garrett turned to her, his mood as lively as her son's.

Hope could see Garrett had already had a shower and dressed in clean clothes. Suddenly, she yearned for the same. "I hate to ask…"

He read her mind. "Take your time."

Hope tried not to wonder what would happen if Garrett continued being this good with Max, and this sexy and appealing, and ultraprotective. "You sure?"

"Yep. I could use the practice."

Once again caught unawares, Hope queried, "For…?"

Garrett shrugged happily. "When I have kids."

SEVERAL HOURS LATER, her shower completed—and vastly enjoyed—numerous media requests and inquiries regarding the scandal all answered and Max down for another nap, Hope joined Garrett in the kitchen, where he was already making dinner.

She watched him prick two russet potatoes with a fork, coat them with olive oil and sea salt and wrap them in foil. "Did you mean what you said about wanting a family?"

"It's why I haven't already accepted the job at Walter Reed in Bethesda."

She took a seat on the other side of the breakfast bar. "Because it means reenlisting."

He slid the potatoes into the oven to bake. "And reenlisting means my orders could change at any time. I'd be sent where they need me. As a single guy, with no responsibilities to anyone other than myself, I've been happy to comply. As a family man, I'd want more control."

Hope had never realized just how tantalizing it was to see a man in the kitchen—until now. Or just how much she had come to enjoy just being with him. "Is that why you haven't married? Because you were on active-duty military?"

"Actually, I was going to get married a few years ago."

Something in her went very still.

It shouldn't have been a surprise. And yet it was. "What happened?"

Garrett poured olive oil and lime juice into a glass baking dish then chopped up fresh oregano, garlic and cilantro and added them, as well. A sprinkling of dried chili powder and cumin followed.

"I discovered there are two kinds of women who don't mind their mates being away for long periods of time." He paused to look her in the eye. "Those who are truly devoted to their men and understand the patriotic need to serve one's country. And those who want the respectability and stability of an official relationship, while still enjoying plenty of time and freedom to pursue other romantic interests."

Ouch.

The sting of betrayal came and went in his eyes.

Heart going out to him, she said, "I'm guessing your engagement fell into the latter category."

He added a slab of flank steak to the aromatic marinade

in the glass dish. "You would guess right." He turned to wash his hands.

"Care to be more specific?"

His shoulders tensed. "My ex is Leanne Sharp."

"Chief of staff of Congressman Jared Thiessen?"

His eyes narrowed. "You know her?"

"I know of her." She was a gorgeous, ambitious Southern belle, from a very well-connected and wealthy Dallas family. Just imagining her with Garrett conjured up a stab of jealousy, which was, Hope knew, completely uncalled for. Whatever they had shared was a one-time thing.

"In my previous job I had a lot of dealings with politicians."

His mouth thinned. "Thiessen?"

"One of his colleagues—Len Miller—had a pretty messy divorce. We enlisted Thiessen, who's public reputation is stellar, to vouch for my client's trustworthiness."

Garrett's expression darkened. "I remember that. You-all spun Miller's infidelity as a domestic dispute, a symptom of the problems in the Miller marriage, instead of the problem."

Which had been true, as far as Hope could discern, anyway. "Len Miller still lost his next election, but I think that had more to do with his voting record, or lack thereof, than his infidelity."

Garrett chuckled grimly, shook his head.

Hope wanted to be let in on the joke. "What?"

His mouth tightening, Garrett turned to get a beer from the fridge. He twisted off the cap, took a swig. "I just find it ironic that you would use *Jared Thiessen* as a moral barometer and character reference."

"Why?" Hope got up to help herself to another glass of milk. Deciding to live dangerously, she stirred some chocolate syrup into it. "Jared's got a great reputation as a family man. Plus, he has won eight straight elections."

Garrett went still.

Hope waited.

Finally, eyes level, he said, "Congressman Jared Thiessen is the love of Leanne's life. She only got involved with me as cover for her affair with him."

Oh, my God. Hope shared his devastation. "How did you find out?"

Garrett began to slice zucchini and yellow squash. "Usual way. Stumbled on some racy texts on Leanne's phone when she asked me to look up our dinner reservations while she put on her makeup."

"That must have been unpleasant." Not to mention careless on his ex's part.

"You'd think that would have been rock bottom." He reached for a couple of carrots and sliced them on the diagonal, added them to the sauté pan.

"It wasn't?"

He turned the heat up beneath the veggies. "She asked me to lie about why we broke up."

"And did you?"

Garrett's face remained implacable. "I saw no reason to hurt his wife and kids. They were innocent and he was a public figure. Had it become known, it would have been all over the news, and the kids would have been devastated."

"So you kept quiet."

Garrett inhaled sharply. "Reluctantly, but yeah."

"Which is why you hate scandal management."

He pinned her with his hard blue gaze. "I hate any hiding of the truth."

HOPE UNDERSTOOD. HE'D BEEN caught in an impossible situation. Still was, in certain respects. His honor was one of the things she loved most about him. "I'm sorry you went through all that."

He snorted in derision. "Live and learn."

Needing to comfort him, she closed the distance between them. Started to reach for him. A knock sounded at the door.

Hope sighed.

He lifted a brow. "Expecting someone?"

"No. Although Lucille texted me earlier and said your brothers might drop by later."

"Doubtful," Garrett said. "At least for tonight. I heard from them, too. Wyatt has a mare in extended labor. Chance is in the midst of re-homing a couple of his prime bulls."

Hope put her hands on her hips. "Well, then."

"I know." Garrett grinned, his usual good humor returning as he strode for the bunkhouse entrance. "I just don't rate." He opened the door.

Darcy Dunlop stood on the other side, a covered dish in hand, a pinched look on her thin face. "Is this a bad time?"

"Not at all." Immediately compassionate, Garrett ushered her in.

Hope smiled. "Hi, Darcy."

"Hi."

"Tank okay?" Garrett asked.

"That's why I came over. To talk to you and give you this." She took the top off the most delicious-looking berry crisp Hope had ever seen. "As a thank-you for helping us out the other night."

"No problem." Garrett looked past her. "I see you got your pickup running again."

"Yeah," Darcy replied nervously. "Smitty's repair shop does a great job."

Garrett gestured for her to have a seat at the counter. "So, what's going on?"

"Tank has stopped going to his physical therapy sessions in town. He was hit or miss before, but this week he's refusing to go at all."

Garrett warned, "He's not going to regain full range of motion with that leg unless he does the work."

"I know," Darcy said sadly. "The physical therapists have all told him that."

"Then…?"

"I think he's starting to give up on thinking things are ever going to get better," Darcy admitted hoarsely. "Anyway, I was wondering, do you think you could come by and talk to him? You were able to make him see reason the other night…" Darcy broke off, tearing up. "If you could do it again…"

"Where is Tank now?" Garrett asked gently.

"Home. His parents went to visit family so we'd have the house to ourselves for a week or so. They thought it would help. But so far, it's just not." Her lower lip trembling, she slid off the stool and backed up. "But I can see I'm interrupting you-all's dinner plans. I should have called first."

If there was one thing Hope knew, it was a person in distress. Crises like this called for immediate action. She looked at Garrett, letting him know with a glance their evening together could wait. He nodded in wordless agreement. Putting a big arm around Darcy's thin shoulders, he said, "Why don't we go see Tank right now."

"You're s-s-sure?"

Garrett nodded.

"Actually," Hope said, "it's a really good time."

Thanks, Garrett mouthed.

He got out the keys for his pickup truck and patted his cell phone. "Call me if you need anything."

She noted he did not promise when he'd be back.

"Will do." She flashed another smile.

Garrett and Darcy left.

Hope finished sautéing the veggies, grilled the marinated flank steak and removed the perfectly baked potatoes from the oven. Although she would have liked to wait for Garrett to return to eat, the fact that she was nursing and still trying to get her milk supply back up dictated otherwise.

So she ate in silence.

Did the dishes.

Nursed Max when he woke up and gave him his evening bath.

Then nursed him a little more for good measure before putting him back to sleep.

And still no Garrett.

She had just finished brushing her teeth and getting ready for bed when she heard the bunkhouse door open and close. She walked out, clad in a pair of pink floral pajamas.

Garrett's dark hair was rumpled, as if he'd been running his hands through it. The faint shadow of an evening beard lined his jaw, circles of fatigue rimmed his eyes.

Resisting the urge to admit how much she had missed him and launch herself into his arms, she asked casually, "Everything okay?"

He sank down on the middle of the sofa, draped both arms across the back, and stretched his long, jeans-clad legs out in front of him. "I talked Tank into going back to PT."

Hope perched in the corner next to him. "Good for you. That will help."

He took her hand in his. Tingles sparked and spread outward, through not just her arm but her entire body.

He smiled. "Physical activity always does."

Feeling somehow unbearably restless, she disengaged their palms and stood. She strode into the kitchen, picked up a near-empty glass off the counter, drained it and set it in the dishwasher. "Did you eat?"

He studied her as she shut the dishwasher door with a snap. Slowly he got to his feet. "Darcy fixed something for both of us."

"Good."

He came closer. Moved around the counter to face her. "Sorry I missed dinner."

The cooking area suddenly seemed awfully small. She crossed her arms in front of her and said seriously, "This was important." Helping people always was.

He nodded. The casual affection in his gaze deepened. He gave her lips a long, thorough once-over. "Not sure most women would understand that."

Oh, heavens, she wanted him to kiss her again. More than that, actually. Hope stepped back. One palm pressed to her head, the other to her waist, she preened like a 1940s pinup girl. "I thought I made it clear." For added emphasis, she tossed her hair, too. "I'm not most women."

Amusement tugged at the corners of his lips. "You might have, at that." He wrapped his brawny arms around her, nuzzled her temple. "Max okay?"

Excitement roared through her and her breath hitched. "He is."

His lips blazed a trail across her cheek. "That's good to hear."

"It is."

He found the sensitive spot behind her ear. Her knees went wobbly.

Hope stopped him, her hands splayed on his chest. The practical side of her knew this was a bad idea. This morning's activities had been reckless enough. She swallowed, determined to enforce at least some limits. "You know this is private."

He stepped back slightly, hands down. "Between the two of us? Of course."

"And only temporary."

Looking impossibly handsome and determined in the muted light of the bunkhouse kitchen, he asked, ever so softly, "Is it?"

Their eyes met, held for several long moments. Her heart pounded and her body pulsed with yearning. "You're headed off to Walter Reed…" Which was much too far away from Dallas.

He stepped forward and closed the distance between them, sending an even higher level of reckless excitement pumping through her veins. "Not necessarily," he said with a shrug. "And definitely not yet."

Chapter Eight

Garrett planted a hand on the counter on either side of Hope and leaned in close enough that she could see the passion gleaming in his eyes. "I realized something today," he told her soberly. "The soldiers most in need are the veterans who are no longer in the military. More has to be done for them."

She wished he didn't look so good, even in jeans, a black cotton polo and boots. She lounged back against the counter, trying not to feel his body heat. "There are existing organizations. Wounded Warriors, for one…"

His gaze roving her upturned face. "And they do a great job. No question. But they can't be everywhere." Lifting his hands, he moved away from her, opened up the fridge and pulled out a beer. "Right now, Laramie County has a growing population of former soldiers. Many aren't physically wounded. But all of them could benefit from more readily available services."

She watched him twist off the cap. Wished she could join him. She poured herself another glass of milk, instead. "Like support groups?"

He toasted her wordlessly. "And physical therapy, taken alongside other vets. Job training. Assistance making the transition into civilian life." He smiled at the intent way she was listening to his plans. "Bess Monroe is doing a great thing in starting West Texas Warrior Assistance. But the Lockhart Foundation really let her down." He shook his head in dissatisfaction. "I'm going to fix that."

She loved it when he was on a mission.

"Singlehandedly?"

Mischievously, he waggled his brow. "I have sway with the board of directors."

Unable to do anything but laugh, Hope quipped in return, "So I've heard." His family did seem to adore him.

She was beginning to adore him.

Especially when he looked at her as if she was the most beautiful, desirable woman on Earth.

He reached up to tuck a strand of hair behind her ear, gazing at her with the same smitten look she had seen other men give their wives in the maternity ward.

"Seriously, I'm going to make sure the dream becomes a reality for the people here in Laramie County, sooner rather than later."

She believed him. Just as she believed he was wildly attracted to her—for the time being. But she had to ask, "How?"

Another lift of his impossibly wide shoulders. "That I haven't quite figured out yet, but I'm working on it."

For a moment, her optimism rose, while her ability to censor her questions failed—big time.

A veil dropped over his emotions. His lips curved ruefully, as if to say, *Let's not get ahead of ourselves.*

Which, really, was what she should have expected, Hope reminded herself. She had no more business weighing in on his career decisions than anyone else in his family.

This was something he had to decide for himself.

"I have a few weeks left, before I have to give the army an answer."

Which begged her next question. Did he know what it

was going to be? The maddeningly implacable look on his face gave her no clue.

"So, at least temporarily, I can stay right here in Texas."

Temporarily being the operative word. Hope pushed aside her selfishness. "Well, that's good," she murmured, forcing a smile. "I'm sure your very philanthropic mother will be really proud of you." As would his whole family.

His sexy grin widened. He put his quarter-finished beer aside, lowered his head and scored his thumb across her bottom lip. "What about you? Are you proud of me?"

A thrill soared through her. Hope caught her breath.

He touched his lips lightly to hers in an angel-soft kiss. Paused long enough to undo the butterfly clip on the back of her head. "'Cause if I'm going to get a gold star for good behavior," he rasped, seductively combing his fingers through the tumbling strands of her hair, "I'd sure like to get it from you."

COMMON SENSE HAD told Hope they shouldn't be doing this again. At least, not while she was still working for his family foundation.

But for now, she thought, as they kissed their way to his bedroom once again, she couldn't think about anything but the closeness she felt whenever she was with him. What was one more moment in time, one more blissful, passion-filled night, except an interlude to be grateful for? And she *was* grateful for the feel of his strong arms around her as he disrobed her, and then himself, and stretched out alongside her on the bed.

Sliding one arm beneath her shoulders, he lifted her head to his. He kissed her temple, jaw, throat. "Have I told you how much I like it when you catch your breath and look at me like that?" He caressed his way down her body, then returned to her mouth and kissed her again, deeply and provocatively this time, the kiss a melding of heat and need. "As if you can't help but want me as much as I want you."

Hope felt treasured in that special man–woman way. To the point that, if she hadn't known better, she would have thought she had finally found the soul mate she had been searching for her entire life.

Maybe love wasn't involved here, but everything else that mattered was present. Which made her feel as if their coming together was a step toward something unconventional—and yet wonderful.

His lips closed over the tips of her breasts. Laved delicately. Sensation warred with the thrill of possession, as he kissed his way lower, across her ribs, her navel, hips. Lower still, he traced the insides of her thighs to the dampness within. His ministrations felt incredibly good, incredibly right. Hope closed her eyes, clung to him and surrendered all the more. The eroticism of his touch flowed over her in hot, exciting waves. Trembling from head to toe at the long, sensual strokes of his tongue and the soothing feel of his lips, she caught his head in her hands and tangled her fingers in his hair. Until, at last, her head fell back; her body shuddered with pleasure. Yearning spiraled deep inside her. And then she came apart in his hands.

He held her through the aftershocks.

"My turn," she teased.

Wanting to take the lead, she shifted positions, tracing the bunched muscles and hot satiny skin, learning the mysteries of him, just as he had come to know hers. Her hair brushed over his ripped abdomen and hard, muscular thighs. Inhaling the tantalizing masculine scent of him, she teased, tormented and pleased. Tasted the salt of his perspiration and the familiar sweetness of his skin. Aware she had never felt so alive, so safe and treasured and loved, she focused on one seductive plateau after another, until he could not help but groan.

Trembling, he reached for her. He shifted her upward, across his body, then over, onto her back.

The warmth and strength of his body engulfed her. She wound her arms around his neck and opened herself up to him, to the sensation of being taken. He lifted her with one hand and then they were one. All was lost in the blazing hot passion and the overwhelming need. Adrenaline rushed. Pleasure spiraled. And in the sweet blissful satisfaction that followed, Hope realized that the notion that she might one day have an adoring husband, in addition to her amazing little boy, and a loving family of her own, was not so far-fetched, after all.

EARLY THE NEXT AFTERNOON, Garrett's only sister breezed through the bunkhouse door. Hope blinked in surprise. "Sage?" This was certainly unexpected!

Garrett came in to stand beside Hope, Max snuggled drowsily in his arms. He bussed the top of his little sister's head. "What are you doing here, little sis?"

Sage set her overnight bag down. "Mom asked me to fly in first thing and meet you all at the ranch. I wanted wheels of my own so I'd have maximum flexibility to come and go as needed, so I rented a car at the San Angelo airport."

"Mom's not here yet?" Chance walked in.

"Actually, she is." Wyatt joined them, with a look over his shoulder at the limo stopping in front of the bunkhouse porch.

Both brothers turned back to Sage and Garrett. "What's going on?" Chance and Wyatt asked in unison.

"No clue," Garrett said.

That made two of them, Hope thought with a twinge of anxiety.

Lucille breezed in. Clad in her usual outfit—a silk-and-linen sheath and heels, trademark pearls around her neck, her hair and makeup expertly done—she managed to look both exceedingly well-groomed and as if she had the entire world sitting on her shoulders.

She was followed by Adelaide Smythe.

Wyatt froze at the sight of Adelaide right behind Lucille. His gaze dropped to Adelaide's rounded tummy and turned dark, then he looked away entirely.

That was weird, Hope thought, wondering what was going on between those two to cause such tension…

Inhaling, Lucille squared her shoulders. "Adelaide and I wanted to talk to you all at once." She paused to make eye contact with everyone in the room. "And we wanted to do it in person."

Which meant, Hope thought, the two women had figured out something…and she had a sinking feeling it had something to do with the annual fly-fishing trip Paul Smythe had secretly skipped this year. The trip he might have taken instead with Mirabelle Fanning.

"We need to have a board meeting," Lucille said, taking her place at the head of the long plank table. "So everyone get what you need to be comfortable, and then have a seat."

Five minutes later, Max was in his port-a-crib, snoozing away, and everyone was gathered around the table, coffee or sparkling water in front of them.

Lucille stood at the head of the table, practically buzzing with nerves. "There is no easy way to tell you this, so I'm just going to say it. Twenty-five million dollars, or half of the foundation's funds, have been embezzled."

The matriarch waited for the reaction to subside.

"All the checks that were supposed to go to the non-profit organizations we were supporting apparently had the 'pay to the order of' information changed, as soon as I signed them."

Another deathly silence fell.

"How is that possible?" Sage asked, upset.

Lucille turned to the forensic accountant.

Face pale, Adelaide explained grimly, "There's a very sophisticated Wite-Out that thieves use on checks that allows them to change whatever they want—the date, the amount, who the money is going to—and still keep the authentic signature of the account holder. On all of the checks from the foundation, only the beneficiary of the check was changed." She swallowed hard. "For instance, Metroplex Pet Rescue became Metroplex Pet Rescue Inc. Meals for Seniors became Meals for Seniors In Need. Preschoolers Read! became Dallas Preschoolers Read! The amounts and dates all stayed exactly the same, which allowed the fraud to go undetected in the Lockhart Foundation ledgers for nearly a year."

"And your father never once caught on to this?" Wyatt asked skeptically.

Hope was surprised, too. From everything she'd heard, she had deduced that Paul Smythe was a very smart man.

Adelaide's voice cracked. "My father did the embezzling."

For a moment, everyone could only stare. Adelaide drew a deep breath, blinking back tears. "Believe me, I didn't want to believe it, either," she said hoarsely.

"Nor did I." Lucille opened up a file and passed around copies of the canceled checks, provided to them by the bank. "But there's no question as to what happened. Paul Smythe's signature is on the back of every single cashed check."

Adelaide nodded sadly. "Lucille and I visited all of the banks yesterday. The various financial institutions where the money was supposed to have been deposited. And wasn't. And the bank where my father used his position as CFO to open accounts in both the fake charities' and the Lockhart Foundation's names, so he could move the money around very easily."

Wyatt shrugged. "Well, if we know all that, can't we get the money back?"

Lucille shook her head.

"It's already been transferred out of the country," Adelaide explained unhappily. "He moved it to a bank in a country that has a no money-tracking agreement with the United States. And then he withdrew all the funds yesterday."

Another tense silence fell.

"Did he do this alone?" Chance said finally.

Adelaide grimaced. "Mirabelle Fanning was a VP at the bank where all the fraud occurred. She managed all the transactions and helped my father open all the bogus accounts. She took a long-planned early retirement last week. We assume they are together."

"Has your father contacted you?" Sage asked quietly, as sympathetic toward her old friend as she was distraught over what had just happened to their family charity.

"He texted me this morning. Said, 'I left the trail so no one else at the foundation would be blamed. Don't bother to look further for the money or me—you'll never find either.' I tried calling him, but his cell phone provider said the account was canceled right after that message was sent. I'm sure he took the battery out and destroyed the phone so there would be no tracking it, either."

"Have you reported all this to the police?" Chance asked.

"No," his mother retorted. "And I don't plan to until after I've personally made this right, visiting every charity in person and paying what is due to them."

"Are we going to have enough money to do that?" Garrett asked, no doubt thinking about the local group that still needed so much help.

Adelaide consulted her computer. "For all but West Texas Warrior Assistance. There, the foundation is going to have to give them what was offered in writing, five thousand dollars, instead of the five hundred thousand that Lucille wanted to give them."

Garrett looked extremely unhappy about that. Hope felt the same. She also knew there was little else that could be done, at least for now.

"And then what?" Sage bit out.

Lucille paused. "I need to talk to Hope in private about that."

"ARE YOU DOING OKAY?" Hope asked Lucille, as the two set out for a walk. The afternoon was hot, but overcast. A stiff breeze blew across the rolling plains.

The older woman adjusted her wide-brimmed straw hat. "I'll be better when I've made my apology and compensation tour."

"Would you like me to go with you?"

"No. I need to handle this alone. Although both Adelaide and Sage have promised to be nearby throughout, for moral support. What I want from you is what we initially discussed."

"A strategic response to what has happened."

"I want to go public as soon as all the reparations are made and we talk to the police."

"There's a chance it could come out before then," Hope warned, but for the moment she let it go. Lucille had enough to do just getting through the humiliating next phase. "What's the chance the money will be recovered?"

"Given the extremely clever way Paul went about all this?" Lucille drew an aggrieved breath. "Next to none."

"I'm sorry about that," Hope said softly.

Lucille turned her attention to the unkempt family ranch land. Although the area next to the bunkhouse had been kept up, the rest of it had not. She sighed. "I should not have been so trusting, old family friend or not."

Hope comforted the older woman the best she could. "Once people know what has happened, and I'll make sure they do, your family will not just be forgiven, you'll all be revered for the upstanding members of society that you are."

"I trust you to be able to handle that."

"And I will," Hope promised.

Lucille turned to look at Hope and said, "It's your ability to convince Garrett to stay in Texas and go along with our contingency plan—should the worst happen and it becomes necessary—that really worries me."

The truth was, it worried Hope, too. When it came to preserving appearances, and/or doing something just because it would look good to outsiders, Garrett had not exactly proved cooperative thus far.

"Have you been able to speak to him yet?"

Guilt flowing through her, Hope shook her head.

Lucille studied her a long moment, which made Hope wonder what the woman sensed. Something, clearly. "Any particular reason why not?" Lucille asked.

Because I was too busy leaning on his big, strong shoulders and making love with him, Hope thought. She drew a deep breath. "I just haven't found the right time to bring it up."

"Laying the groundwork?"

"Trying to develop a rapport."

Lucille considered that. "Makes sense."

Did it?

Up until now, Hope hadn't considered her attraction to Garrett would make it impossible for her to do her job well. But that was exactly what was happening.

Fortunately, she could fix that. "I'll find the right way to broach it with him, if and when the time comes," she reassured Lucille.

She was still hoping it wouldn't, because the Lockharts had been through enough.

"See that you do," Lucille said. "Because the future of the foundation and our family are depending on both of you."

AN HOUR LATER, Sage and Adelaide had departed for Dallas. Chance and Wyatt had also gone back to their ranches—but not before Garrett asked them for a favor that he hoped would be well received by Tank and his wife.

In the meantime, he needed to find out what was going on with Hope. She hadn't looked him in the eye since she had left the emergency board meeting and gone off to confer with Lucille in private. "What were you and my mother talking about for so long?" Garrett asked.

Hope carried her laptop over to the table and powered it on. "Plans to rehabilitate the foundation's reputation. How and when we're going to announce our findings. What comes next, once all previous commitments have been met."

He sat down opposite her at the table and kicked back in a captain's chair. "What does come next—especially if half the money is gone? Has my mom told you what her plans are?" She hadn't told any of them.

Hope paused. *A-ha*, Garrett thought. She did know something she was reluctant to share.

Finally she looked up from the computer screen. Her

green eyes lasered into his. "There are too many variables right now to figure that out. What we do know is that anything could happen, and most of it will likely be extremely damaging, at least initially. Which is why I'm staying behind to put together a film that will introduce your mother to the public."

Hope wasn't easy to read when she was in work mode. "What do you mean? My mother's been a fixture on the Dallas social and philanthropic scenes for years."

Hope made a note on the pad next to her, then tucked the pen behind her ear. She leaned back in her chair. "But that's all they know about her, Garrett. What they see in news clips on TV or in the papers." She paused to let her words sink in. "They see photos of Lucille stepping out of a limousine, or pictures of her gorgeous mansion in Dallas. They don't know how the family charity came about, or why she and your father wanted to do this in the first place."

Hope shook her head in mute frustration.

"They don't know where your mother and father grew up, or how life was for them in the beginning. Or how generous and loving your mother is—deep down." She leaned forward urgently. "We need to shed light on that so people understand that none of this was deliberate, that Lucille's heart was, and still is, in the right place."

"So your primary goal remains…?"

She regarded him stoically. "To do what I was hired to do and save the foundation first."

Which meant what, exactly? Garrett wondered, growing alarmed. His family and his mother were second? All he knew for sure was that once again Hope wasn't quite meeting his eyes. Never a good sign. He stood, shoving the chair back so abruptly it scraped across the wood floor. He stood, legs braced apart, hands on the table in front of him. "Tell me you're not planning to throw my mother under the bus."

"The media and gossip sites have already done that." He opened his mouth to argue, but she lifted a staying hand. "However, at the end of the day, the only people who should bear the brunt of the blame for this are CFO Paul Smythe and banking VP Mirabelle Fanning. Before all that information is made public, though, we have a lot to do. Which is why," Hope persisted, all kick-butt scandal management expert once again, "I need the *complete* co-operation of you and your brothers for the next few days."

FOR GARRETT, THAT started with a trip to town to meet with Bess Monroe the following morning. To say the West Texas Warrior Assistance organizer had mixed feelings about receiving a check for only five thousand—instead of the agreed-upon five hundred thousand—dollars was an understatement. So Garrett did what he could to make the situation better, which in his view wasn't nearly enough. He stopped by the grocery store, got plenty of milk for Hope and enough food for a few more days, then headed back to the Circle H.

Hope had Max in her arms, her phone headset on. She was pacing back and forth on the porch, trying to keep Max entertained while she spoke.

"…That's right. It's not common knowledge…Because Lucille Lockhart doesn't want anyone to know. But I know how fair you are in your reporting, and I thought you should be aware…As we speak! Yes, the checks are going out… No. Lucille doesn't want to formally announce until every organization has been paid…Of course. I think a sit-down could be arranged here at the family ranch. Maybe the day after tomorrow?…Thanks. You, too."

Hope swung around to see him standing there. A guilty flush crossed her face.

He had only one thing to say to her.

"What's going on, Hope?"

Chapter Nine

Garrett set the groceries on the kitchen counter with a thud. He had shaved before going into town, and the tantalizing fragrance of his aftershave still clung to his jaw. His dark hair was tousled. He had on worn jeans and an untucked dark blue shirt that brought out the intense sea blue of his eyes. "I thought you weren't going to throw my mother to the wolves."

Determined not to put herself in an emotionally vulnerable position with him, especially when it came to the foundation work, she said, "I'm not."

He strode closer, clearly trying to intimidate her. "Then?"

She feigned immunity to his disapproval. "Lucille called while you were out. Half an hour ago, the foundation's attorney received a demand letter from a lawyer representing fifteen of the charities." Keeping her voice low, she shifted Max a little higher in her arms so he could look out over her shoulder. "They're threatening to sue."

Garrett's gaze darkened as the information sank in.

"Apparently, it's going to be an exclusive for KTWX on the eleven o'clock news. Which is why I called my contact at rival KMVU, and told her the promised payments had been going out all afternoon at the foundation offices, and would be completed by 5:00 p.m. tomorrow."

"And my mother approved this."

"I spoke with her at length, while you were in town. She understands that we have to make it clear she was doing the right thing *before* she received the threatening demand letter. Otherwise it looks as if she only followed through because she was facing legal action. Which brings me to the next thing we need to discuss…the personal check you wrote to West Texas Warrior Assistance."

As she moved closer, Max reached out and put a tiny fist in the short sleeve of Garrett's shirt. Ignoring the tender look he threw her son, Hope swallowed through the dryness of her throat and prodded, "In addition to the five thousand dollar check you were to deliver from the foundation."

His expression quickly became veiled. He squinted. "How did you know about that?"

Easy. "Bess Monroe wrote your mother an email, thanking her and citing your generosity. Your mom was impressed, by the way."

So was she.

"Don't make a big deal out of it," he told her gruffly. "And don't even think about putting what I did in any press release."

Luckily she hadn't thus far. Mostly because she had wanted to speak with him first and find out what had prompted him to be so generous, when she knew from Lucille that he and his siblings lived only on what they were each able to bring in, which in his case was his military salary. She watched as Max fisted his other hand in Garrett's shirt. "Why not?" Figuring she might as well let Max have what he wanted, she transferred her little boy to Garrett's waiting arms.

"Because it's not really charity if anyone knows about it." Despite the tension hovering between them, Garrett flashed a heart-melting grin at the baby cuddled against his chest. "It's grandstanding for attention."

Tenderness drifted through Hope at the sight of her son's blond head nestled against Garrett's chest. "My grandmother used to say that."

"It's true."

Hope began putting groceries away. "That sentiment must put you at odds with the new family business."

Garrett lounged against the counter. "I think what my father and mother wanted to do was great."

Spying an opening for the job Lucille wanted her to do, Hope said offhandedly, "Ever thought of joining the foundation? Maybe as the new CEO?"

His brows lowered like thunderclaps over his gorgeous blue eyes. "No."

"It could help." She stood on tiptoe to put the cereal on the appropriate pantry shelf.

She felt his glance rove her bare legs, the trim lines of her skirt, blouse. "Ask Adelaide."

Her body warmed everywhere his eyes had touched. Hitching in a breath, Hope worked to keep her mind on the problem at hand. "Can't. Optics."

His gaze locked on hers. "Sins of the father...?"

"Something like that," she answered, flushing self-consciously. "It's best, at least for now, that Adelaide stay well in the background of any story on this. The last thing she needs when pregnant with twins, and absorbing her father's betrayal, is to be hounded by the press."

"True."

"So, back to the sit-down your mother is going to do here the day after tomorrow. The bunkhouse is great. We can film in here, but we'll also be taking a tour of the land, and we can't have the ranch looking so unkempt overall."

"It's already been taken care of," he informed her. "Chance

and Wyatt are bringing over their farm tractors first thing in the morning. Tank and a couple other rehabbing vets are going to mow all the grass and pastures. They need the work and we need it done."

Wow. He was really on the ball. "Does Bess Monroe know this, too?"

Garrett grimaced. "I didn't mention it. I'd appreciate it if you didn't make a big deal out of it, either. These guys have had their manhoods wrecked by their injuries. They don't need anyone painting them as charity cases, because they're not."

"Got it, Captain."

Looking relieved, he turned Max around so his diapered bottom was resting on Garrett's forearm, his back to Garrett's chest. His tiny little hands curled around the wrist stabilizing his middle.

Max blinked at Hope. Smiled.

She smiled back at her son.

"Are you done working for the evening?"

Hope shook her head. "As soon as I nurse Max again and get him down for the evening, I'm going to work on the practice Q&A for your mom. She has to rehearse for the TV interview."

Garrett's gaze narrowed skeptically. But for once he had no ready remark.

"It will be much easier for her if she feels prepared," Hope explained.

He quirked his brow. "And to do that…?"

"I'll write the questions Lucille's liable to be asked and then print out the answers she needs to memorize."

"Sure you don't need to make up some cue cards for her, too?"

Here at last was the sardonic man she had met on the plane. "That will come later."

He did a double take. "I was kidding."

"I'm not." Deciding she had been ensnared in Garrett's keen blue gaze far too long, Hope turned away. His increasing discontent was not her problem when she had a job to do. "We're also going to make a short, interview-style video of our own to put up on YouTube and the foundation website. That way we'll be able to make sure that everything that needs to get said will get said, in exactly the way it should be."

"And here I thought the overly scripted part of my family's life was over," he muttered. He looked at her long and hard. Loathing the suggestion she was somehow creating a fake tableau, she stared right back.

He exhaled roughly. "Guess not."

Carefully he transferred Max to her, spun around and walked out the door.

AN HOUR LATER, Garrett met his brother Chance at the office building he owned. His younger brother elbowed him in the ribs. "I thought you'd be making time with Hope tonight."

Garrett flipped him off. "Funny."

Chance needled him with a long look. "Sure seemed to be something happening between the two of you earlier today."

There had been. Until Hope had gone back to manipulating events to ensure the outcome she was determined to have.

Then something in Garrett had gone cold.

The last thing he wanted was to spend more of his life worried about how everything appeared on the surface, rather than what should be going on deep inside. He'd had enough of that in his childhood and when he was engaged.

He wasn't going down that road again. Not professionally. And definitely not personally.

Garrett unlocked the door and strolled inside. "Next thing I know you'll be saying we were communicating without words."

Chuckling, Chance joined him in the small, outdated lobby. "Weren't you?"

"Keep it up and I'll tell you where you can put your asinine observations." Garrett switched on the lights.

Chance laughed all the more. When Garrett declined to join in, his younger brother finally slipped into general contractor mode. "So, what were you thinking of doing here?"

Garrett was surprised to hear himself say, "Gutting it and renovating it instead of selling it, as is, for pennies on the dollar."

"Keep going." Although he made his living raising and investing in rodeo bulls, Chance still earned money on the side, the way he had before he'd gotten into ranching, by doing home repairs and remodeling work.

"I want to take the elevators out of the center of the building and move them over to one side. Have two of them, instead of three. And make them look like the freight elevators you have in lofts, with a cage door on the front."

Chance made notes. "It could be done. What else?"

"I'd like the first floor to be completely open. On the second and third floors, I'd like to have four private offices and a larger meeting room."

Chance looked up. "I'm assuming you already have a tenant in mind."

Which was, Garrett knew, in some respects even crazier for someone who wanted to cut ties with his past in Texas. Being careful to keep a poker face, he nodded. "I know some people who might be interested, if the work was done in advance. So can you get me an estimate?"

"Sure thing. What are you going to do about the Victorian?"

Another dilemma. One he hadn't expected. Garrett said gruffly, "I have to clean it up before I can do anything with it."

Chance's gaze narrowed thoughtfully. "And then…?"

Garrett rubbed the tense muscles in his neck. "Still thinking."

"Might not hurt to keep it for a while. As a home base, for when you visit."

And remember how Hope's eyes had lit up in wonder and delight the first time she walked through it with him?

Tensing, Garrett said, "Or not."

"Have you had any offers on that?"

"Just a call from Molly Griffin, that local interior designer and general contractor. She offered to redo it for me, if I wanted to make a little money on it."

Chance groaned. He scrubbed a hand over his face. "Do us both a favor and don't listen to Molly Griffin."

"Do I detect a little emotion there, brother?" Now this was interesting…

Chance scowled. "Just take my advice."

"Why?"

Another grimace. "Because she's a social-climbing pain in the ass."

Ah. Garrett shook his head at Chance. "Well, so long as you like her, then…"

"I. Don't."

"Now who doth protest too much?"

This time, Chance flipped *him* off. Garrett laughed despite himself as the two brothers walked out together.

"By the way, that was a pretty nice thing you did for the West Texas Warrior Assistance program," Chance said, when they reached their pickup trucks.

Garrett bit down on a string of oaths. Was nothing private around here? "How did you hear about it?"

His baby brother grinned and slapped his shoulder amiably. "In Laramie County, good news travels fast."

THE LIGHTS WERE on in the Circle H bunkhouse when Garrett turned the borrowed pickup into the driveway around 11:00 p.m. The blinds were pulled.

Inside, Hope was clad in a pair of thigh-length white cotton shorts that showed off her long legs to perfection and a loose-fitting pink cotton camp shirt. The sleeves were rolled up past her elbows. Her feet were bare. A blue cotton burp cloth had been thrown over one shoulder and Max had both his fists resting on her shoulder. Wide awake, with milk bubbles on his lips, he was looking around. He smiled when he caught sight of Garrett and bobbed his sturdy little body up and down excitedly.

Hope turned, a welcoming smile on her face.

If she was still piqued from their slight tiff earlier, Garrett observed, she wasn't showing it as she patted her son's back, nuzzling his blond head.

To his surprise, he found his irritation with Hope gone, too. The time-out from each other had helped. So had the realization that in a temporary hookup, which was what Hope kept insisting this was, each individual's values didn't have to line up the way they would in a successful permanent arrangement. In a fling, all that mattered was for a couple to have fun hanging out together, and they did, and have an even better time in bed. Which was also where they really clicked.

Work never factored into it.

Nor did their long-term wants, needs and expectations.

So there was no reason they couldn't continue to enjoy each other's company in the short amount of time they had left at the ranch.

Hope glanced at Garrett, admitting ruefully, "I think Max expects rocking up and down like this will actually launch him where he wants to go."

It certainly appeared that way, Garrett thought with amusement as he crossed the room to their side.

Max pushed up harder.

Hope's smile widened. "Do you mind holding him for a second? I'm trying to warm his bottle for him."

"Sure."

No sooner had Garrett shifted Max onto his shoulder than a loud burst of air escaped. Hope wrinkled her nose at the odor of digesting milk.

"Or maybe not…" she said. "Given what he's about to do."

The smell emanating from the diaper area told the whole story. He slanted her a glance. "You think I'm afraid of a little poop?"

She propped her hands on her hips. Lifted her chin. "Aren't you?"

Garrett knew when he was being tested. "Nah. Best he get it out now. Otherwise, it will wake us all later."

Hope wrinkled her nose. "True."

He glanced at the work spread out over the plank table. It appeared she had been as busy as he had.

"Still writing the Q&A?"

As much as he was loath to admit it, he figured it was necessary. His mother always felt better when she had a script to follow.

"No," Hope said cheerfully. "I finished that a few hours ago." She chuckled as her son balled up his fists, turned red and worked on his task with a few healthy grunts.

"Ah, the joys of parenthood," he teased.

Hope groaned and shook her head. "You have no idea..."

He was beginning to get one, though.

Garrett watched as she tested the baby formula on her wrist, then, still finding it lacking, put the bottle back in the bowl of warm water.

She ambled closer. The increasing odor had them both wrinkling their noses.

"Sure?" she teased, holding out her hands, as if to take Max. "It's not too late to change your mind."

This was all part of having a kid in your life. To his surprise, he liked every moment, even this. He would really miss Max when he was gone.

Max's mommy, too.

If he were honest...

Which was why he should keep things nice and casual between them.

He gave a wry smile. What better way to keep the romance out of the situation than by dealing with a little stink? He stared at her, deadpan. "To show you what a trouper I am, I'll even change his diaper."

Hope's merry laughter filled the bunkhouse. "This I have to see."

She accompanied them to the makeshift changing area she had set up on the sofa. Garrett laid the infant down on the thick, waterproof pad. Keeping hold of Max, the way he'd seen Hope do, he sat down, too. The snaps that ran down both legs of Max's sleeper were easy to undo. Same with unhooking the sides of the diaper.

He peeled it back. Dared a peek. Couldn't help but groan right along with Hope.

It was so gross.

"You can still bail," Hope challenged him.

"Nope." Garrett lifted the little boy off the mess, folded the messy diaper in half, put it aside and set Max back down on the waterproof pad. "I'm doing it. Aren't I, Max?"

Garrett plucked the wipes out, one after another, carefully cleaning until Max's entire diaper area was as clean as a whistle. Which wasn't exactly easy, since Max kicked his legs and feet the entire time and tried to grab the soiled wipes with his little hands.

Hope hovered. "You've got a little spillover on the changing pad…"

"I've got it." Using more wipes, Garrett cleaned that, too. And then Max's little hands and feet, for good measure. Satisfied all was well, he slid a fresh diaper beneath the baby, fit it against him, just the way he had seen Hope do dozens of times in the past week, then fastened the tabs. The sleeper got snapped up, too, although that took a moment to figure out. "Now you can have him while I go wash my hands," Garrett declared proudly.

"Good job, *Dad*," Hope teased.

Dad?

Funny, he liked the sound of that, unexpected as it was to hear.

Her hand flew to her mouth. "I'm so sorry," she rushed on. "I don't know why I said that. I must be getting a little punchy."

Or you just have your defenses down.

He paused to let her change places with him. He shrugged off her mistake matter-of-factly, for both their sakes. "It's probably because I've been acting like one…"

"Or because Max doesn't really have one." Hastily, Hope gathered her now fragrant-smelling son into her arms. "So no one currently has that title, which is why it was okay to make a joke, because I wasn't taking anything away from anyone else."

He stared at her in surprise as her face flushed bright red. He had never imagined she could be so embarrassed. "You really don't have to spin this, Hope," he said gently. "I'm not offended."

Flattered, maybe. Crazy as that sounded. But not offended. Nope. Not offended in the least. Still ruminating on the reasons behind her Freudian slip, Garrett went to the kitchen sink and lathered up well.

Hope followed him. "Okay. Because I—" she tipped her head up to his, Max still gathered against her breasts "—I really do appreciate everything you've done for us the past few days. From buying groceries to taking us to the hospital, to holding Max and giving him a bottle and changing his diaper."

He had pretty much done it all.

Aware she looked as if she felt she and Max had imposed on him, Garrett waved off her guilt. "You've been helping my family. I'm helping yours. It's the way the world works."

"Or should," she said, a slight catch in her voice.

Another silence fell, more companionable this time.

Max looked at the bottle of milk. He gave a little lurch. "Meh…meh…"

Garrett took it out of the warm water, wiped the outside dry then tested it on Hope's wrist. "Perfect," she said.

He handed it to her and she settled on the sofa, Max in her arms, and began to feed him. But not before he'd gotten in a few more hungry cries.

Garrett settled beside them, observing softly, "It almost sounds like he's saying *Mom, Mom*, instead of *meh, meh*."

"I know." Hope smiled tenderly, admitting, "I can't wait for the day when he really does call me that."

The question was, would he be around to witness it? "It won't be too long," Garrett predicted, leaning close enough to breathe in the baby powder scent of them both.

Hope sighed wistfully. "Actually, it will be months from now, according to the developmental timeline."

Months.

Would he even recognize Max by then? He knew how much babies could change in appearance as they grew the first couple of years. The differences were even more significant when you weren't seeing the baby every day, the way he was now.

He forced himself not to think about that.

Or grow maudlin—as Hope looked about to do.

After all, no permanent decisions had been made.

Garrett tucked his little finger into the center of Max's fist, grinned when the baby gripped it tightly. As if he didn't want to let Garrett go any more than Garrett wanted to let Hope and Max go.

"Yeah, well," Garrett predicted gruffly, pushing the unwanted emotion away, "I think Max is so exceptional he'll be way ahead of that."

Hope beamed. "I do, too."

They exchanged grins.

In that moment, he saw the faint shadows beneath her eyes that even makeup couldn't hide. He thought about the fact that she still wasn't making enough milk and that the prescription for that was a healthy diet and lots of rest. The latter of which she definitely had not gotten today.

"You look a little tired," he told her, not sure if it was the lover in him or the physician doing the talking. "Want me to finish feeding Max while you get ready for bed?" So she and her baby boy could drift right off to sleep?

Hope mistook his suggestion. The color came back into

her cheeks. "Oh, I'm not headed for the sack," she said firmly, squaring her slender shoulders. "At least, not anytime soon."

Chapter Ten

Well, that made two of them making stupid verbal slips tonight, Hope thought in chagrin.

Drawing a deep breath, she tried to pretend her mind hadn't immediately gone in the same direction as his the minute bedtime had been mentioned. When the racing of her pulse, the innate desire to make up for their little tiff earlier in the sexiest way possible, said otherwise.

Aware he was still assessing her intently, Hope forced a smile. "I have several more hours of work to do, minimum, before I call it a night. But…" Being careful not to dislodge the bottle of formula from Max's mouth, she handed over her son. "If you want to feed Max for me, I really would appreciate it."

Garrett shifted the little boy against himself and settled on the sofa, one brawny arm resting on the cushioned end, Max snuggled against his chest. "No problem." His mood just as purposeful as her words had been, he continued giving her son the bottle.

Was he just doing this to make up for how short he'd been with her earlier? Maybe. He was a mature adult. He knew she was just doing her job. That she was who she was, just as he was who he was. They would never share the same view about how necessary appearances were in life. Never mind whether or not they should be manipulated to secure an outcome.

She'd never be as blunt as he was.

And he sure as heck was never going to be anywhere close to discreet.

It didn't mean they couldn't be friends, Hope rationalized, doing her best to protect both their hearts.

And interim lovers…

All she and Garrett had to do was accept that whatever was going on with them was only temporary, and take it day by day, moment by moment.

That would certainly lessen the overall stress of the situation. And wasn't that what she was all about? Choosing the path of least conflict? For everyone?

OBLIVIOUS TO THE tumultuous nature of her thoughts, Garrett looked up at her as Max's feeding slowed down. Seeming no more anxious to revisit their earlier tiff than she was, he asked curiously, "What was Max drinking earlier? When I came in?"

When Max had still had frothy white bubbles on his lips. Once again, Hope had to work not to appear self-conscious. "Breast milk."

"Then, if he was just fed a few minutes ago…?"

"I didn't have enough."

His glance went to her breasts.

Her nipples immediately tingled, but not because she didn't have enough milk.

Funny, he hadn't noticed the loose fit of her blouse. But then, he'd been too busy looking deep into her eyes…as if trying to figure out what to do about the hopelessly intimate situation they'd let themselves get into.

Hope swallowed. "I could have put Max back to bed, but I knew he was still a little hungry, so if I had gone ahead and put him down he would be up again in two hours. On the other hand, if he gets as many calories as he needs now, even if takes a little longer to feed him since he's not as intensely interested as he was a little while ago before he had the edge taken off his hunger, he will probably sleep a good six hours."

"Six hours? Really?" Once again, Garrett looked as interested as any proud daddy.

But he wasn't Max's daddy.

And would never be.

She needed to keep reminding herself of that.

Hope moved away from the compelling sight of Max snuggling up to Garrett.

So Garrett was not just strong and protective, he was also laudably tender, too. So what? It didn't change anything between them. *Couldn't.* And if she let herself imagine otherwise, they'd both be in big, big trouble. "He slept that long last night," she reported, trying to distract herself by tidying up the kitchen, emptying out the plastic bowl and putting it in the rack to dry.

"But, again, that's what is on the developmental schedule." Hope paused to dry her hands. "I think the only reason Max wasn't doing it before this was because he was growing and wasn't getting quite enough nutrition from my breast milk alone to help him sleep through the night."

Garrett's eyes tracked her every movement as she walked around the breakfast bar. "So you're okay with combination feeding now?"

Hope settled in front of her computer once again. "I'm beginning to see the beauty of it." She pulled her chair up. Elbows on the table, she rested her chin on her folded hands. "I also realized I don't have to be so hard on myself. As a mom, I don't have to do everything perfectly. I just have to try to do my best."

The upward curve of his masculine lips was as encouraging as the gleam in his eyes. "I'm glad."

Once again their glances meshed, held. Once again Hope wished she wasn't working for his mother and the foundation. That the two of them could put everything else aside and just be together like this.

But she *was* working for the Lockhart Foundation.

And she had a job to do if she was going to protect Lucille and the family's reputation the way she had promised. So, without another word, she turned her attention to the computer screen and went back to work.

GARRETT HAD BEEN wondering if a formal apology for their earlier disagreement was warranted.

She'd quietly indicated it wasn't.

Now, as she immersed herself fully in her work, he had to wonder if he'd read her mood correctly, after all. Frustration formed a knot in his gut.

How was it he had just ended up in the confusing morass of his youth? With everyone surreptitiously working to protect each other's feelings, appearances of civility reigning supreme and no one saying what they really meant or felt?

Suddenly, the idea of reenlisting in the military, where everything was short and to the point, seemed a lot more appealing than it had just twenty-four hours before, when he'd been wrapped in Hope's arms.

Maybe his earlier self-assessment was right.

He just wasn't cut out for this.

With a decisive frown, Hope picked up her laptop and brought it over. She settled beside him, close enough so he could see the screen while still giving their tiny chaperone his bottle.

She picked up a throw pillow and wedged it between

the two of them. So she could rest her elbow on it while she worked? Or to ensure they wouldn't physically touch?

He didn't know the answer to that.

However, he *did* know she still smelled like lavender baby powder and the vanilla-scented hand soap she favored.

They were both, he noted, very soothing fragrances.

Max, opening his eyes to grin up at his momma, seemed to think so, too.

Hope spared her son a sweet smile, causing Garrett's heart to lurch painfully in his chest, then went back to the task at hand, explaining, "I'm still trying to put together the backstory on the foundation. Not the abbreviated one that's on the Lockhart Foundation website, which tells us virtually nothing about your parents except that they are rich and want to do good."

"Wow. That's harsh." But true in a way he never would have expected an exceedingly tactful woman like Hope to come out and say.

"I know. It doesn't begin to cover how the foundation came about. And I need that."

"Why?"

She scooted as close as the pillow wall she had built would allow. "Because of this." She clicked the split-screen function. Eight different windows popped up. He read the titles of the stories out loud: "'Lockharts Try to Get Ahead of Potential Lawsuits.' 'Too Late to Do Good?' 'Boxed Into Giving, as Charities Revolt.'" He exhaled roughly, a muscle pulsing in his jaw. "Wow. I thought you said that leaking the information about what my mom is doing ahead of the eleven o'clock news would diminish the bad publicity."

"And it has." Hope clicked on another screen of multiple headline windows. "This is where we started."

He continued to read. "'Lockhart Foundation Stiffs

Charities.' 'Lockhart Foundation Turns Its Back on Needy.' 'Nonprofits Tell the Ugly Truth about Lockhart Foundation Largesse.'"

Looking more accepting of the situation than he felt at that moment, Hope explained, "We went from all bad publicity to a press that is doubting whether your family and the foundation is bad or not. The next step is to take those doubts as an open window or door, and give the public another glimpse of who your parents really were when they started out and how their largesse all came to be."

"Makes sense." Noting Max had pushed the nipple all the way out of his mouth, Garrett set the bottle of formula aside and shifted Max upright, so the baby could look over his shoulder while working up a burp.

Hope tucked an errant strand of honey-hued hair behind her ear. "So I've asked your siblings, and now I'm asking you as well, to tell me what you know about the family history. Sage sent me photos from her computer, of the ranch as it was when your mom and dad were growing up here in Laramie County."

Frank and Lucille stood in front of what then had been a sturdily built split-rail fence. The barn, painted red at the time, was behind them. Grazing cattle and horses could be seen in the distance. "They look so young." So…Western. Both were clad in worn jeans, plaid shirts, boots and straw hats.

Hope clicked on the keyboard. A new image appeared on the computer screen. "Here's another of them in their first home in Dallas. One of them standing in front of the Lockhart Asset Management office. Another of them with all five of you kids when you were in elementary school."

He nodded.

Their clothes were sophisticated, haircuts just as perfect. And yet…

"None of you look very happy in these pictures." Hope pointed out with a frown. "Which is why I asked Sage to find me some more photos of you-all having a good time."

Garrett reflected on that. Noting Max was starting his baby push-ups again, he slid his palm a little higher, to rest between the little fella's flexing shoulders. "I'm not sure there are any."

Hope's elegant brow furrowed. "That's what she said. Can you tell me why that is? So I don't accidentally open up a can of worms?"

"You want to know what it was really like when I was a kid?"

She nodded.

Garrett sighed heavily. "Dad was wrapped up in building up his hedge fund. He worked constantly—he was almost *never* home. My mom was always on the board of some charity or organizing some black-tie gala to help further the family's social connections." None of whom were apparently rallying around his mother now, he couldn't help but note. "All us kids were enrolled in private schools only the most elite of the elite could get into."

Garrett flicked a glance her way. "I always liked the academic challenge of school. Especially science and history." Which had led to his career in the military and medicine.

"Were you happy?" she asked quietly, her eyes lighting up with interest as she held his gaze.

Yes and no. "I wish there had been more of a connection between us," he admitted finally. "In the military, you work as a team. There was no teamwork in my family growing up."

"I see that now."

He wished she didn't look so beautiful in the late-night light of the bunkhouse, wished he still didn't want to make love to her quite so much. "We all became closer when my dad was diagnosed with his heart problems. We had time to reevaluate our lives before we had to say goodbye to him."

Max lurched and let out a loud burp.

Hope's proud grin matched his own.

A little amazed at how quickly he had become adept at feeding and caring for an infant, Garrett turned Max back around and settled him against his chest.

Enough with the questions about his childhood.

"What about you?" he asked Hope softly. "Your family? You've never said much about that."

He wanted to know all about her, too, he realized.

For a moment, he thought she wouldn't answer.

Head ducked down, so he couldn't see into her eyes, she watched him offer Max the bottle again. "I was an only child. My parents own an extended-stay hotel for the very wealthy."

"In Houston," he remembered.

"From an early age, I was expected to keep out of the way and, when I got older, to work as hard as possible to keep our well-heeled guests comfortable. Most of them were in some sort of personal crisis, due to relocation, home renovations that were lasting forever, nasty divorces, stuff like that."

"That doesn't sound…pleasant," he sympathized.

She shrugged. "I saw how people could 'spin' things, which in turn made their lives better, their crises a little less daunting."

"That's when you decided to go into public relations."

An accepting smile turned up the corners of her lovely lips. "It wasn't that hard of a leap to make. I already knew how to deal with highly emotional and volatile people, and not lose my own cool."

She was certainly good at handling the members of his family; they all adored her. In fact, they seemed willing to do anything for her. As would he. "Are you close to your parents now?"

Another short intake of breath. Hope fixed her stare on a painting on the wall. "I love them."

"That's not the same as being close."

Hope turned her glance to Max, who was drowsily sucking on the bottle. She reached over and tucked her little finger into his tiny fist.

The action had her forearm resting against Garrett's chest. He liked the feel of that. Even better was the fact that she didn't immediately pull away from the cozy physical contact.

"Do you and your parents not get along?" Garrett asked. He could understand that, too.

There were times when he and his mother still irritated the heck out of each other. Usually because his mother was surreptitiously pushing him to do what she wanted him to do, not what was right for him, in his view.

Hope sighed. "My parents were always extremely critical." She shook her head, the pain in her eyes matching the pain in her voice. "There was simply no pleasing them." Her shoulders rose, then fell. "I disappointed them even more when I didn't join the family business."

"They must be proud of your success now."

"Yes." Seeing Max had, indeed, gone to sleep, she put her laptop on the coffee table, gathered her son into her arms and carried him into the bedroom.

When she returned, she settled on the sofa, removing the pillow she had previously put between them. Looking as weary as he expected her to be, at that time of night, she stretched both long, lissome legs out in front of her and propped her slipper-clad feet on the coffee table. Her head fell to rest against the back of the sofa. Noting how exhausted she seemed, how in need of comforting, he stretched an arm on the sofa behind her, and pulled her closer, into the curve of his body. Sighing blissfully, she rested her head on his shoulder, then she picked up the conversation as if no time had elapsed. "Yes, my parents are proud of my professional success," she said.

"But...?" he sensed there was more.

Her slender body tensing, Hope snuggled closer. His pulse took another leap at the effortless way their bodies aligned.

Hope sighed. "They didn't like the fact that I had a baby on my own. Or the fact that I got fired for being involved with a British reporter, after the scandal with the ambassador's son was resolved. They wish I'd move back to Houston, take a place nearby and raise Max there."

"I'm guessing that doesn't fit in with your plans?"

Her expression wistful, she admitted, "I do want him to have family. More than just me."

He could understand that. It was a lot to raise a child on your own. Still keeping her tucked in the curve of his body, he reached over and took her hand in his. Gratified, her fingers tightened in his. "But...?" he asked, just as softly, guessing there was a caveat.

She gazed down at their clasped hands, said fiercely, "I don't want him to ever grow up feeling like he is in the way, or somehow less than people who have more money, or feel criticized at every turn, like I did."

Garrett understood that. He wouldn't want that for either Hope or Max, either. "Okay, then," he said gruffly, bringing her closer still, wishing he had the power to make all their dreams come true.

"What *do* you want for you and for Max, ideally?"

WHAT DO I WANT? Hope thought, her emotions getting the better of her once again. *You in our life.* But aware it was way too soon to say something like that to Garrett, when thus far all they'd had was a tentative friendship and a fling that would likely end when he reenlisted and took the job in DC, she ducked her head and fibbed, "I don't know."

Garrett shifted her over onto his lap. Hand beneath her chin, he lifted her face to his so that she could not help but look into the mesmerizing depths of his eyes.

His smile was slow and sensual.

"How about this?" He lowered his head and kissed her in a way that was tender and provocative. Hope's lips tingled. Lower she felt a burning desire between her thighs. And still he seduced her with his lips and tongue, as if he were on a mission to fulfill her deepest wishes, to provide an intimacy that included everything but commitment and pure romantic love.

She drew back on a long, lust-filled sigh. Doing her best to contain her out-of-control emotions, she said, "I think you know the answer to that."

She did want to make love with him. Beyond that, she didn't know. But maybe she didn't have to think, she realized as he slid his hands to her waist and brought her flush against him.

Maybe she didn't have to be perfect.

As he had said, he hadn't hired her, so there was no conflict of interest between the two of them. All he wanted was to make love with her, and all she wanted and needed was to make love with him, too. This time, not as the result of some kind of crisis with Max. Or because they needed to discover if the first time was as good as they thought it had been. But because they were getting closer.

Pretending a great deal more detachment than she felt, she moved off his lap and said breathlessly, "Just to be clear." Because her legs felt wobbly, she settled on the sofa next to him once again. She turned toward him, so her bent knee nudged his rock-hard thigh. "You know this is still just a fling... That work still takes precedence?"

Was she speaking more to herself or to him? Who was she warning here? Garrett wondered.

His body thrumming with need, he drew her to her feet. He tangled one hand in the spill of Hope's hair. The other slid down her back, settled against her waist.

"I know we're headed into forbidden territory," he whispered roughly against her mouth.

And, as far as that went, it was fine with him. He didn't care what fibs Hope had to tell herself. As long as they came together like this, found more to life than either had been experiencing. His body igniting, he felt her melt against him.

"I know I want you." He kissed her again, until her breasts rubbed up against him, as did the rest of her from shoulder to knee. Needing more, he danced her backward to the wall, grinding his hips against hers until the hard ridge of his arousal pressed against the softness between her thighs. She trembled as they kissed. And shuddered even more as he divested her of her shorts and relieved her of her panties.

Her lips softened beneath his and she clung to him, her hands slipping beneath his shirt to caress his shoulders, back, spine. Able to feel how much she needed and wanted him, he opened her blouse and bra, slid between her thighs, pulled both her legs to his waist and set about exploring even more.

Joy pulsed through him. Her head fell back as, eyes closed, she gave herself over to his tender ministrations. And only when she was wet and ready did he step back long enough to drop his trousers and roll on a condom.

She leaned against the wall, their eyes locked, the air between them charged with excitement. She beckoned him close, running her hands over the hard muscles of his thighs, the curve of his buttocks, the small of his back, before coming back around to cup the weight of him in her hot, smooth palms. Stroking, learning, tempting. Fierce pulsing need swept through him as he pressed up against her, lifting her, positioning her as kiss followed kiss, caress followed caress. And still it wasn't enough, not nearly enough.

Needing to possess her the way he had never possessed any woman, Garrett wrapped her legs around his waist, and smoothly moved up, in, pushing his erection into her trembling wetness, until they fit together more snugly than he could ever have imagined.

She cried out and fisted her hands in his hair. "More..."

Arching against him, her hands slid down to his hips. Once there, she directed him to move with tantalizing slowness. Then faster, deeper. Filling and retreating. Finding meaning in every breath, every kiss, every sweet, hot caress. Until at last everything merged. Passion and need, tenderness and surrender. She met him wantonly, stroke for stroke. Satisfaction rushed through them, and there was no more fighting the free-falling ecstasy that warmed their hearts and filled their souls.

GARRETT THOUGHT THEY might call it a night and retreat to his bed, to sleep wrapped in each other's arms until Max woke, needing to be nursed again.

Instead, Hope disengaged herself from him almost immediately and slipped away. When she returned, she was wearing another pair of summery cotton pajamas. Her hair had been pulled back, her makeup washed off.

She was ready for bed, all right, but she couldn't have been more businesslike as she retrieved her laptop computer. "What was your favorite memory as a kid?"

Garrett strode off to his bedroom. He returned in his

own nightwear, a pair of jersey running shorts and an army-issue T-shirt. "Tell me you're not still working."

She gave him a look. "You know I am."

She had warned him.

So why was he surprised?

Aware it was getting harder and harder not to spill his guts to her every time they were together, he went to the kitchen and plucked a crisp apple out of the fruit bowl. "Tell me you're not going to use any of this in your narrative."

She watched him take a bite of the sweet, delicious fruit. "Only if you give me permission."

Their eyes clashed. The closeness they'd felt when they were talking earlier and making love faded.

Garrett strolled closer, persisting, "I get to review everything that pertains to me and my family."

"Okay," she agreed from her place at the long plank table.

Garrett took a chair at the end, kitty-corner from her. "When I was a little kid, every once in a while my mom and dad would bring us out to visit my Grandpa Lockhart at his family ranch, the one where my brother Wyatt now lives."

Briefly, Hope consulted her notes. "The Wind River Ranch."

"Yes."

Her head lifted and her green eyes locked on his. "You did a lot of cowboy stuff?"

Exhaling sharply, he found himself wanting to be the stuff of her fantasies. "Yes and no." Summoned memories came flooding back. "Grandpa Lockhart was career military, so he spent more time showing my brothers and me how to defend ourselves and survive in the wild than how to wrangle a calf. But there was just something about being out in the countryside—small towns, in general. It was so different from Dallas."

"Sounds like you almost got emotionally attached to a part of the Lone Star State," she teased.

Garrett kicked back in his chair. "Maybe to all the military lore…it sure made me want to follow in my grandpa's footsteps. Anyway, Grandpa Lockhart died when I was ten, and my mom and dad sold the Wind River Ranch, the way they had sold my mom's family ranch, and put the money into expanding Dad's company. So we never came back until my dad got sick, when they told us they'd been out here, buying property in Laramie County, not just for themselves, but for all of us."

Hope typed a little more, then paused to look up at him. "It sounds nice."

He finished chewing another bite of apple. "I guess it was, as far as gestures go."

Hope rested her chin on her hand. "You think that's all it was? A gesture?"

He wasn't sure what she was getting at. "What else could it have been?"

"Chance and Wyatt live here now."

"Only because they had already been working as cowboys and always wanted to ranch. Zane and I…"

"Are military through and through?"

Two weeks ago, he would have said, yes, he was. Now…

Now that he'd spent time with Hope, he wasn't sure what was true.

She went back to typing data into her computer, even more fiercely. Finally, she paused. Narrowed her gaze. Surveyed him, head to toe. As aware as he that he still hadn't answered her. Mostly because he had no reply to give. Just yet.

"Does this mean you decided not to reenlist and take the slot at Walter Reed in Maryland?"

It means I don't know. And until I do...

He got up to throw his apple core in the trash, hesitating only long enough to wash his hands and get a drink of water before striding purposefully back to her side.

Decision made, he took her by the hand. Pulled her to her feet. "Enough questions."

Her breath caught audibly. "Garrett! What...?"

Figuring that the only way he could give either of them any peace at this moment was to make love to her, he wove his hands through her hair, lifted her lips to his. "It's late," he told her, kissing her until her knees went weak and she kissed him back just as passionately.

"There's only one thing we need to do now," he growled, breathing in the sweet, womanly scent of her and swinging her up into his arms. "And that's go to bed."

So they did.

Chapter Eleven

"Since when do you walk around with a baby strapped to your chest?" Chance asked Garrett the following morning.

Garrett adjusted the white sunhat on Max's head, making sure the infant was shielded from the harmful rays while still able to view all the activity. And there was a lot to see.

In the fields surrounding the ranch buildings, two large tractors were being operated by Tank and one of his rehabbing veteran friends. As the chest-high weeds disappeared, the smell of fresh-mown grass hung in the hot summer air.

"Since Hope only got about two hours of sleep last night," Garrett replied.

Some of which had been his fault. They had spent a couple of hours, total, making love.

The rest was all on her.

Chance asked sympathetically, "Max giving her a rough time?"

Garrett shook his head. "She was working on a revised written history of the formation of the Lockhart Foundation. Putting together some photos, making plans for the camera crew coming out today and tomorrow."

"They are everywhere, aren't they?" Wyatt said, joining them.

Garrett blew out a frustrated breath. "Not to mention

constantly underfoot." Taking both video and still photos of the ranch entrance, the mown and unmown fields, and the barns, corrals and original ranch house.

"And what's with the 'staging' being done in the bunkhouse?" Wyatt asked, not nearly as irritated as Chance to find interior designer/general contractor Molly Griffin there.

Garrett turned so Max could get a better view of the tractors. "Hope wanted some more Texana feel to the main room."

Chance chuckled. "Well, if that's the case, I could probably borrow some stuffed animal carcasses for the wall."

Garrett spared a glance at his younger brother. "I think you know what Hope probably would tell you to do with that suggestion."

Chance shrugged. "I know what *you* would tell me to do. Hope is a lot more polite."

So true.

"Although she can be direct," Chance said. He turned to Wyatt. "Did she ask you to bring over some horses?"

Wyatt nodded affably. "I said I'd give her one tomorrow morning, before the TV crew arrives."

"She wanted cattle from me but changed her mind when I said all I had was bulls," Chance drawled.

The brothers all laughed.

"Has anyone heard? Is Mom coming back tonight?" Chance asked.

"Yes," Garrett said. "If all goes according to plan. She's been meeting with the charity CEOs in groups at the foundation office to speed up the delivery of the money. It appears once word got out on the news yesterday, everyone clamored for their money before it all ran out. So at least that part of wrapping up this whole mess will be done with."

Wyatt frowned. "What about the police?"

Garrett informed them, "Her attorneys are handling that for her. She'll eventually need to be interviewed by detectives, of course, but that can wait a few days."

Molly walked out of the bunkhouse. She attached flag holders to two of the front posts, then hung an American flag on one and the state flag of Texas on the other.

Garrett frowned.

So did his brothers.

Paying homage to their homeland was a very good thing. But as a means to an end…?

Temper rising, Garrett eased the baby carrier off his shoulders. He looked at Chance. "Mind walking this little fella around for me for a few minutes?"

Chance shrugged. "As long as he doesn't mind."

Because Chance was nearly the same size as Garrett, little adjustment was needed to the Baby Bjorn carrier. The sleepy Max frowned at the transfer, then paused, looking up at Chance.

Chance mugged comically and talked gibberish in a soft, soothing tone.

Max grinned.

Unable to resist, Garrett slapped his brother's shoulder. "Just so you know—it's only gas."

"Ha!" Chance crowed. "He likes me, don't you, Max?"

Chance and Wyatt walked over to the shade, still doting on the baby. Garrett headed inside the bunkhouse. Hope was on her smartphone, video chatting with his sister Sage. "Thanks so much. I'll be sure you get all the groceries you need…Yes. Promise. See you tonight." Hope hung up. Immediately concerned, she asked, "Where's Max?"

"With Chance and Wyatt. He's fine." Garrett gestured to the window.

Hope peered out. Smiled. "For not being used to men, Max sure is adapting easily to this environment."

Too bad I'm not, Garrett thought sullenly.

Hope studied him. "What's wrong?"

WHAT WASN'T? GARRETT HISSED out a breath, feeling as if he had been transported back to his youth. "For starters—" he gestured broadly "—all this."

Her emerald eyes widened. "You don't like the new vases filled with wildflowers?"

If only it were that simple. "I don't like false impressions."

She put her hands on her hips. "We're just sprucing things up a little bit, doing what Lucille would have done had she been here."

"You're making it look like something it's not. This isn't the true current state of the Circle H." Perpetrating another myth would only make the family reputation shakier. And while he couldn't have cared less what anyone said about him, this stuff did matter to his mother. Garrett strode closer, noting Hope looked exhausted, too. "Any good reporter could find a local resident to complain about the prior state of the ranch. Go on record as saying all this was only done for the TV interview."

Her chin lifted. "You'd prefer it be filmed looking run-down and unkempt, which is the shape most of the property is in?"

"Why film anything here at all? This is a zone of privacy, or it should be. Why not film in Dallas, at my mother's home there, or at the foundation offices where things could easily stay just as they are?"

Hope glared at him. "Because all of those places have negative connotations for the viewing public. They support the image of your mother that has been exaggerated and bandied about in the press. None of them show where she came from. Or how she and your father eventually discovered that money didn't bring them happiness, but giving to others, bringing their whole family back to their roots, did." Hope came closer. Another shimmer of tension floated between them. "It's a great story."

"Then why can't you just tell it openly and honestly instead of doing all this?" he asked her in frustration. "It's bad enough that you're writing advance questions and answers for my mom to rehearse with, and inviting a friendly journalist to cover the story." He shot her a disapproving look. "Which, by the way, I'm still not totally on board with. Remind me again why it's so important?"

Hope dug in all the more. "Because I think Lucille'll be more comfortable if she feels *prepared* rather than under siege." Clearing her throat, she added, "Of course, there is a way to make this easier on her..."

"Just issue a press statement and leave it at that?"

"No. One step better."

He waited.

"Your mom could step down as CEO."

Shock turned to anger that Hope could even suggest it. "Not. Going. To. Happen."

Her jaw took on the consistency of granite, too. "Have you spoken with Lucille about it—even in theory? Because I have to tell you, it's the best way to take the heat off her."

"No. And for the record, I don't want you or anyone else suggesting it to her, either."

For a moment, he thought she was going to argue the point. Cheeks pinkening, she stepped closer and, dropping her voice persuasively, tried another path. "Have *you* thought about taking a more active public role in managing the scandal?"

Garrett blinked at her in surprise. She was serious! He

flexed his shoulders in an effort to make the increasingly unsettled feeling go away. "Such as...?"

"Heading up a task force?"

He couldn't help but laugh. "A little silly when the foundation only employs three—I guess now, two—people. My mother and her executive assistant, Sharla."

Hope lifted a delicate hand. "Again. It's all about optics."

He leaned over, until they were nose to nose. "And again. I'm not."

She stared up at him. Shook her head. Sighed. "Substance over style?"

The way she said it made it seem like a character flaw. "You betcha."

Hope paused again. She seemed to be wrestling with something. Finally, she sighed again, sifted both hands through her soft blond hair and said, "Look, I can see all this is bothering you."

You think?

"So why don't you take a break from it. Go off and find a way to relax, do something you like. I can interview your brothers this afternoon, get what we need for the revised family history from them."

R & R sounded tempting. Leaving her alone with his two very single brothers did not.

Although they had a rule about not going after the same woman, Chance and Wyatt did not know he'd staked a claim where Hope was concerned. Although they had sensed his interest, he couldn't tell them anything definitively because he had promised Hope he would keep their fling a secret between the two of them.

Although that, too, was a misnomer in his opinion.

"Well?" Hope prodded impatiently.

Garrett snorted. "Not sure you'll get anything you can

use from Chance or Wyatt." *Except maybe embarrassing stories about yours truly.*

"Mmmm." She considered for a long moment, then met his challenge with a level glance. "I bet I can." Her gaze softened. "Seriously, your mom and Sage will be back late this evening."

"Adelaide...?"

"Is staying in Dallas to help the police try and track down her father and Mirabelle Fanning."

That sounded like Adelaide. Responsible to the core. Which meant this scandal must be killing her, too.

"So you have plenty of time to take a time-out from all of this redecorating chaos, and enjoy what little R & R you have." She patted his arm. "In the meantime, have a little faith. And trust me to be able to put together a video perspective that does ring true."

"Trust me", Hope had said.

Did he?

Personally, Garrett thought, the answer was yes. When it came to anything one-on-one with him, he did trust her. But when it came to her doing her job, it was a different matter entirely.

There, he found it a lot rougher going.

Aware, however, that he couldn't do anything about that—he hadn't hired her, couldn't fire her—he decided to tackle something he could accomplish. Getting the Victorian cleared of all trash so it could be put on the market.

He worked through the rest of the morning and the entire afternoon without taking a break. The physical activity felt good. But not as good as seeing Hope walk through the door at dinner time, a pizza in one hand, a six-pack of flavored water in the other. She walked past him to the window seat overlooking the backyard and set both down.

Hands on her hips, she turned around, first scanning the newly cleared-out downstairs, then him. Taking in the fact that he was shirtless, she smiled and quipped, "Too bad I'm not looking for studly actors to star in a soap commercial."

"Studly?"

She waved an airy hand. "I've been around horses all day."

"Plural?"

She sauntered closer. "Wyatt said since I declined all of Chance's bulls that he would bring me two horses, instead. They're really gorgeous, by the way. Your brothers put them in the corral between the bunkhouse and the barns."

Her hair shone like gold in the sunlight pouring through the windows. He itched to run his hands through it. "I thought the corral was in bad shape."

Shaking her head, she raked her plump lower lip with her teeth. "Chance brought some cowboys over and they fixed it. Put on a new coat of paint, too."

It was odd not to have their tiny chaperone. 'Cause right about now, he needed a chaperone to keep from following his base instincts. He put a twist tie on the trash bag he'd been filling. "Where's Max?"

"Bess Monroe came out to the ranch to film a pro-foundation bit for me, then offered to watch Max while I went off chasing you."

Was there anyone she couldn't charm into doing her bidding? "You could have called me on my cell. I would have watched him for you."

"I needed a break from all the action, too." She sat on the counter while he washed up as best he could with the hand soap and paper towels the renters had left behind. "Missed a spot." She pointed to his chin. He gave it a swipe. "Still missed." She pointed again.

"Third time's the charm." He gave it another try.

Eyes darkening, she smiled. "Or maybe not." She leaned over and did it for him.

He looked down at her. She looked up at him.

He had the feeling she wanted to make love with him as much as he wanted to make love with her.

But, once again, duty called.

She pushed off the counter and walked over to retrieve the roll of paper towels, the pizza and the flavored water. There was no comfortable place to sit inside, so they took everything out to the back porch and settled on the steps that led down to the spacious yard. "I'm guessing you brought me dinner for a reason?" he asked dryly.

She handed him a slice of pepperoni pizza and a paper towel. "I did want to talk to you."

He uncapped a chilled beverage for them both. Taking a cue from her serious expression, he said, "I'm listening."

"I had a phone call from your mom a little while ago. She wants to shut down the foundation entirely. And make the announcement tomorrow afternoon."

Garrett enjoyed a bite of the hot, delicious pizza. "Makes sense, if all the money is gone."

"Does it?" Hope sighed. "We don't know for certain that law enforcement *won't* be able to recover the twenty-five million that was stolen. If they do…"

"In cases like this, it's always a long shot."

"But it happens, Garrett." She helped herself to a slice, too. "We shouldn't rule that possibility out."

Garrett arched a brow. "Nor should we push or guilt my mother into doing something she doesn't want to do anymore."

Hope pushed on in a surprisingly empathetic voice. "That's the thing. Lucille's not really in any position to make a decision like this right now. There's too much going on. Too many emotions. Too much shame and embarrassment."

She paused to look into his eyes. "Your mom hasn't had a chance to feel the accolades for what she has managed to do, for the last two years, the last week. There's still a lot she *could* do, even if she doesn't have anywhere near the financial resources."

Hope had a point. There was no reason to rush into or out of anything. Not the family's involvement with the foundation. Not his connection to Hope and Max, either.

"That's why you asked Bess Monroe to come and talk about West Texas Warrior Assistance, isn't it?"

"Yes, that's right," she said, nodding. "They need a lot more than what they have to meet their goals, but a little can still go a long way to get them started. It's going to be good publicity for WTWA. And, when your mother sees the video clip, I think it might give her a fresh perspective on the goals yet to be achieved."

"So she won't quit. And you won't have failed in your mission to save the foundation."

"Right."

"I still think it should be my mother's decision. I'll back up whatever she wants to happen."

Hope studied him as though he was a test she just had to pass. "Even if it's not what you want?" she asked finally.

Aware he'd been cut out of the loop in some bizarre way, and Hope hadn't been, Garrett grimaced. "Even then."

BY THE TIME they'd finished eating, the last of Hope's dwindling supply of energy had seeped from her body. And it was only six thirty in the evening. How was she ever going to make it to Max's bedtime?

"You look tired," Garrett said, ruffling the hair on the top of her head.

She leveled him with a look. "Thanks."

He smiled at the sarcasm dripping from her voice. He wrapped his arm about her waist as he walked her to the curb, where her SUV sat parked behind his truck. "Why don't you let me drive you back to the ranch?"

Resisting the urge to curl up against him and take a good long nap, Hope fished the list and keys out of her bag. Now was not the time to lean on her military man. "Can't. I have to stop at the grocery store to get stuff for Sage to cook for the film crew and reporter tomorrow."

Garrett read over her shoulder. Swore at the lengthy and, in some cases, rather complicated ingredients.

Hope gestured aimlessly. "She's a chef."

"She's impossible."

Hope made a face. "I'll tell Sage you said so."

Garrett tweaked Hope's nose. "She already knows. I'll help you get the supplies. "

"I'd appreciate that. Bess said she could stay as late as nine o'clock, but I'm anxious to get home to Max."

By the time they hit the checkout line, Hope was yawning.

Garrett pushed the basket full of groceries out to her SUV.

He gave her another long, assessing look. She lifted a palm. "Not to worry. I may not be able to have coffee, but I can have a cup of ice chips. Chewing on those while I drive will keep me alert just as well."

With a frown, he headed for the Dairy Barn next door. "I'll get it for you."

Hope stifled another yawn. "You are a prince among princes," she called after him.

He turned and flashed her a sexy grin. The kind that said he'd accept payment for his kindness later.

With an amused shake of her head, she climbed behind

the wheel, let her head fall forward onto the wheel and closed her eyes, just for a minute. It had been a mistake to spend time making love with Garrett the night before instead of using all available hours to sleep.

She could have gotten four hours of rest instead of just two. But she had wanted to be with him, so she had been. Besides, it wasn't as if she hadn't gotten by on even less sleep in times prior, when working in crisis mode.

It was only a few more days and then the scandal would be winding down. And then she'd be able to sleep as much as she wanted, she thought, as darkness descended around her.

Chapter Twelve

"Please stop asking me that. Everything is *fine*," Hope insisted agitatedly, for the third time, twenty minutes later.

Except clearly it wasn't, Garrett thought, as he drove them back to the ranch. "Are you angry because I woke you up?"

"Of course not." Resting her elbow on the SUV window, she shaded her eyes with her hand. "I couldn't just continue to sleep in a grocery store parking lot. Not when I have Max waiting and so much work to do."

He got that she was frustrated and embarrassed. But why unleash those emotions on him? Unless she somehow blamed him, too. For predicting she might doze off behind the steering wheel? For being there to protect her? For making love with her when she should have been bypassing their budding relationship and working, in her view?

And it *was* a relationship, even if she wouldn't yet admit it.

Still trying to coax a smile out of her, he teased. "Even if there had been a way to move you out of the driver's seat without rousing you, I'm not so sure it would have been good 'optics,' me lifting a quietly snoring woman out of one area of the car and stowing her in another."

Hope turned to him in sharply waning forbearance.

Irked to find them so completely out of sync, he surrendered. "Okay. Bad joke. You weren't snoring, loudly or otherwise. But…" Maybe it was better they get her emotions out in the open. Let whatever was bothering her surface, so they could deal with it. Together. He slanted her a deliberately provoking glance. "You do agree you were in no condition to drive?"

Hope shook another ice chip into her mouth. "You were right, okay?" she snapped finally. "I was too tired. I screwed up. And you win. Okay?"

No, it wasn't okay, he thought, as she continued staring out at the pastures dotted with cattle and horses, and the occasional goats or alpacas. And it hadn't been about winning. Or losing. Just safety. Pure and simple. That, and maybe his overwhelming need to take care of her. A need she now seemed to reject.

This, after accepting his assistance for days now, however and whenever she needed it. Garrett wondered if sleep would help. "You can close your eyes, if you want," he said softly.

She turned and gave him another long-suffering look that made him want to take her in his arms, hold her close and kiss her until her unprecedentedly grumpy mood passed. Her patience clearly at an end, she shook her head in silent remonstration. She sighed, pulled out her phone and punched in a number.

Maybe it was post-pregnancy hormones.

Knowing better than to suggest that, however, he paused at an unmarked intersection then turned onto the country road that led to the Circle H.

Listening, Hope smiled. "Hey, Lucille," she said with a sudden burst of cheerful energy. "We're almost there… Yes! As soon as I arrive. How's Max?" Hope listened some more, smiled again, then ended the call.

Maybe that was it.

Maybe she just missed her little boy.

To his knowledge, except for the first day they'd met, this was the first time she had been away from Max in a week. He could see where that would upset her.

After spending most of the day away, he missed the little tyke, too.

A minute later, he turned into the lane and drove up to the Circle H bunkhouse. His brothers had already left for their own ranches, to see to their herds. Inside, his mother, sister and Bess Monroe waited.

Hope said hello, then headed down the hallway. "Just let me peek in on Max…"

"He is such a sweet boy," Lucille said, her yearning for grandchildren of her own more evident than usual. Hope tiptoed back out. She went over to give Bess Monroe a hug. "I can't thank you enough."

Bess beamed. "My pleasure. Besides, I owe you for all those great ideas about how to get the WTWA message out there so we can ramp up the fund-raising."

"Let me know if I can do anything else." Hope encouraged, walking Bess out. The two women stood talking for a moment. Hope returned to the house while Bess drove away.

"You helped Bess, too?" Garrett asked. The last time he had seen Bess, she'd still been pretty frustrated with the whole situation. Now, thanks to whatever Hope had done, she seemed optimistic about the organization's fate.

Hope nodded. "It's a really good cause. I'm going to help them in any way I can."

"The foundation will, too," Lucille said.

Garrett glanced at his mother. "I thought you were closing the foundation, as of tomorrow."

Looking simultaneously bone weary and amazingly strong of will, Lucille waved off the suggestion. "Hope and Sage both helped me see that was simply a reaction to all that's occurred. Of course we're going to keep the foundation going," she said stubbornly.

All three women exchanged smiles.

Garrett suddenly felt as excluded as if he had wandered into a No Boys Allowed club.

Hope gestured toward the table. "Ready to see what we've done?" she asked Lucille.

His mother gave a little smile, even though she was as pale with fatigue as Hope and Sage were.

This was ludicrous, Garrett fumed. It was nearly nine thirty. Everyone there had been going nonstop for days now. Hope and his mother, in particular, both had deep shadows under their eyes and looked like they were about to keel over. Someone had to save them from themselves.

"This can wait until tomorrow," Garrett said firmly. He pointed to Hope and his mom. "You two both need to go to bed."

Both women looked at him as if they had no idea who he was. And did not want to know.

"Tell me you did not just say that," Hope muttered.

As the head of the family and the man who cared deeply about all the women in the room, he stood his ground. "Sleep deprivation causes all sorts of serious health issues."

Sage was amused. And apparently amenable to reason. His mother and Hope were not.

He tried again. "If you won't listen to me as your son—" he stared down Lucille, who stood in solidarity with Hope "—or your..." He paused, looking at Hope. She lifted a brow, practically daring him to go on.

No way was he falling into that minefield of trying to put a label on what they had, when what they had was—at Hope's insistence—completely private. At least for now.

Once the scandal was resolved, he would see about that, too.

He shoved both his hands through his hair, aware he had never felt so aggravated. "Listen to me, ladies—*as a physician*, then. Left untreated, sleep deprivation can wreck havoc with every system in the body…"

Lucille interrupted, before he could go on in harrowing detail, "So can the stress and tension of important work left undone."

He blinked at his mother. Who was this woman who had been Go Along to Get Along his whole life?

Garrett turned back to Hope, who seemed to be the only person in the room Lucille was listening to at the moment. "Help me make her see reason," he gritted out.

To his surprise, Hope shook her head. Just as quietly defiant as his mother, she looked him in the eye. She retorted, "You're the one out of line here. So maybe it's you, Garrett, who needs to go bed."

PRIVATELY, HOPE KNEW Lucille was exhausted to her bones. She also knew the impossibly generous matriarch would spend another night, lying awake, worrying, if she did not see how much progress had been made remaking the foundation's image while she had been off making good on the financial promises of the Lockhart Foundation.

So, ignoring Garrett's fierce disapproval, she led Lucille and Sage over to the long plank table and sat down side by side with them in front of her laptop.

Hope pulled up the history of the ranch. The video montage and voice-over had been set to an orchestral arrangement of one of Lucille's favorite songs, "The House that Built Me."

Lucille put her hand over her heart, as the old black-and-white photos of the Circle H and of her childhood appeared on-screen. She caught her breath at the sight of the flags of Texas and the United States. Eyes glistening, she confessed emotionally, "When I got here tonight, and I saw the flags on the porch, the way they used to be when I was growing up, I was so happy I nearly burst into tears."

Hope smiled. There was no doubt from the photos she'd seen, and the stories she'd heard, that the Hendersons of Laramie County had been a very patriotic family. "I noticed them in the photos."

Lucille pointed to the bunkhouse, as it had been, years prior. "This photo was taken when my parents and I still lived here, instead of in the ranch house that was built later. Once we moved into that house, Dad hung our flags there." She shook her head. "It always meant so much to us. Dad being former military and all."

Out of the corner of her eye, Hope saw Garrett's look of chagrin, followed swiftly by apology. And on top of that, regret that he'd never noticed what she, as an outsider, had quickly seen.

Hope went through the rest of the video history, showing Lucille and Frank's humble beginnings, his business success, their rise in Dallas society and the start of the family's charitable foundation.

"We're going to use that to show how this all began."

"It's perfect, Hope. So much better than what has been in the press."

They still had work to be done.

"I'd still like to rehearse the Q&A, but if you're amenable, we can wait until tomorrow morning to do that," she said.

Lucille nodded. "You're right. We're all exhausted."

Abruptly, Max let out a cry signaling he was waking and needed to be fed. Hope smiled. "If you-all will excuse me..."

She stayed in her guest room to nurse. When she emerged forty-five minutes later to dispose of a soiled diaper, no one was up but Garrett. He followed her outside to the garbage cans. "I owe you an apology."

Hope stood for a moment, admiring the warm summer breeze and the deep black sky overhead. A full moon shone down upon them. "I misunderstood about the flags."

She pivoted to face him. "Obviously."

He continued soberly, "And I probably shouldn't tell you what to do."

She arched her brow. "You definitely should not tell me what to do," she reiterated as warmth spiraled inside her.

His expression gentled. "You worried me."

Hope sighed and met his eyes. "I worried myself," she admitted. "I've never done that, fallen asleep at the wheel."

He laid a comforting hand on her shoulder. "The car wasn't on."

"Still." She bit her lip. "If you hadn't gone to get ice…" The tears she'd been holding back clogged her throat. She drew another deep breath and tilted her face to his. "What would happen to Max if something happens to me?"

The next thing she knew, Garrett's arms were around her. He pulled her against his solid warmth.

"Nothing is going to happen to you," he told her gruffly.

With him there, beside her, she could believe it.

The problem was, he wasn't always going to be there to protect her, and/or Max. And when that day came…

More tears flowed down her face.

"It's okay," he soothed, holding her close. "I'm here."

And he stayed with her, until she caught her breath and and turned her face up to his. As grateful for his assistance as she was embarrassed over her own shortcomings.

Tenderness radiated in his gaze. "What else do you need?" he asked her softly.

Hope gulped, still too shaken up and too worn out to censor herself. "For you to hold me," she whispered, as a new wave of emotion swept over her.

"That, I can do," Garrett promised, wrapping his strong arms around her.

Holding her close.

Until she finally accepted his wordless urging and got into bed. He climbed in beside her, curling his big body around hers, protecting her as she drifted into a deep, much-needed sleep.

GARRETT WOKE JUST after six the next morning. He reached for Hope, but to his disappointment found the bed beside him was empty. The bunkhouse was exceptionally quiet. He found Hope sitting on the back porch, still in the clothes she'd had on the night before. She was seated on the glider, Max in one arm, bottle feeding him.

She cast him a beleaguered glance. "Don't start. My milk supply is low."

He moved toward them. "I wasn't going to say anything." Even though they both knew she needed more sleep than she was getting. Or had been getting for the past week.

"Good." She turned her attention to the sun rising in the east. A warm breeze ruffled her mussed, golden hair. Like last night, she was near tears. Mostly, he figured, of fatigue. "Because it wouldn't have been well received."

And with good reason, he thought. Hope was definitely still highly irascible and incredibly beautiful, despite the dusky shadows beneath her eyes.

Aware she seemed as fragile emotionally now as she had on the ride back from town the previous night, Garrett moved the stack of black-and-white photos and résumés she had spread out on the cushion beside her. He sat down. Max immediately propped a sleeper-clad foot on Garrett's forearm and stopped drinking from his bottle long enough to make flirty eyes and smile.

Affection flowing through him, Garrett smiled back.

Max resumed sucking down his breakfast, his innocent blue gaze moving from Garrett to Hope and back again.

"So what are you doing?" Garrett indicated the photos printed off her email.

"Looking for my new nanny. The agency is trying to pair me with a replacement for Mary Whiting."

"She isn't coming back at all?" This was bad news.

Hope released a shaky breath. "Her mother needs her, so she is taking a part-time position close by."

Garrett fanned through the applicants, trying to find the bright side. "All of them look nice."

Hope sighed. "Not to mention impossibly well trained. British nanny academies are the best."

"Then…?"

Hope's lip took on a troubled curve. "Something could happen to the next baby nurse—or her family—too. I don't want Max getting attached to a series of people. And his stranger-danger phase is coming."

He blinked in surprise.

"All six- to nine-month-old children go through it," Hope explained seriously. "Just as they usually start experiencing separation anxiety at nine to twelve months."

She never ceased to amaze him. "Did you memorize that?"

She blinked. "Doesn't everyone?"

Garrett draped his arm along the back of the glider. "I have no clue."

She settled into the curve of his body. "Well, they should."

He cuddled her close, drinking in the vanilla and lavender scent of her. He pressed a kiss to the top of her head.

"What else is bothering you? And don't try and fib. I can tell something is really upsetting you."

Hope studied the golden sun rising slowly in the east then, settling even closer, looked up at him. "What if I do get another nanny and keep working these ridiculously long hours and Max bonds with someone else more than me? Because, let's be honest, Garrett—" she paused to look deep into his eyes "—life would have been a whole lot easier the last week if I hadn't had to cart Max everywhere with me. And fit his feedings in between work sessions."

Garrett studied the anguished expression on her face. Finally they were getting to the root of what had been upsetting her on the ride back from town the previous night. "Yeah, but the week would have been really dull without Max, too. I know for a fact every one of us has enjoyed having the little guy around." *Me, especially.*

"Yes, well, that's because right now Max thinks that everyone is his friend. It was why I was able to leave him with Bess, and Wyatt and Chance yesterday for a little while."

Garrett snorted. "That also explains why Max took so readily to Chance and Wyatt yesterday."

Hope shifted toward him once again, her shoulder bumping his. "Speaking of your brothers… Do you know they wouldn't let me put Max down at all yesterday? They took turns wearing the baby carrier and passing Max back and forth." She shook her head in astonishment. "I've never seen two guys so over the moon." She gave Garrett a closer look. "Do all the men in your family have baby fever?"

Garrett exhaled in exasperation. "Don't lump me in with my cowboy brothers." *Especially when it comes to you and Max.*

"Please," she scoffed. "You've got the most acute case of baby fever of all!"

Noting it was time for Max to burp, Garrett held out his hands. "That's just 'cause Max is so darn adorable."

Smiling proudly, Hope shifted Max to his arms. "He is, isn't he?"

So was his momma. It didn't matter what she wore, or didn't, or what time of day it was. She was absolutely gorgeous, Garrett reflected. He couldn't stop looking at her.

A comfortable silence stretched between them.

Max burped loudly and grinned, then patted his hand against the side of the bottle as if to say *more, please*.

Hope handed Garrett the baby bottle. He settled Max in the crook of his arm, aware he could get very used to all this. It was definitely affecting his future plans.

But it was too soon to discuss all that.

That he knew.

"So," he said, turning the conversation back to something they *could* discuss. "No more British nannies?"

Hope lifted one hand. "I have to find some sort of child care because I have to work to support us. But I also need an arrangement that has very flexible work hours." She shook her head miserably. "You've seen how crazy it can be when I'm in the midst of trying to manage a crisis."

Hers was a demanding profession, for sure. He searched for a solution, and finally pointed out, "You get paid well enough to take fewer jobs."

Her delicate brows knit together. "It doesn't really work that way. You're either available at a moment's notice or you're not. Clients in the midst of a breaking scandal have very little time. They're not going to waste it calling someone who has a reputation for possibly not being available due to child-care issues."

He shrugged. "You could hire someone to assist you at Winslow Strategies."

"I'd have to train them, bring them up to speed. Again,

something I don't have time to do right now. And care for Max. Plus..." Her lower lip trembled and her voice trailed off in distress. "What happens if I'm at work when Max turns over for the very first time and I miss it? Or takes his first step? Or says *Momma* instead of *meh-meh-meh* when he wants to eat?"

Able to understand that—it was something he had ruminated over, too—Garrett tucked Hope into the curve of his arm. "It could still happen, anyway."

Scowling, Hope shifted so her breast pressed into his chest. "Whose side are you on, anyway?"

"Yours. And Max's. Always."

She sighed, slightly calmer.

He loved the way she felt cuddled against him. Tenderness flowed through him. Daring her wrath, he pressed another light kiss to the top of her head. "Sure you don't want to go back to bed?"

Hope rolled her eyes. "We have a house full of family, in case you've forgotten."

He liked the sound of that. *We.* Who would have thought? A week ago, all he'd wanted to do was avoid family. Now having everyone nearby felt really good.

He turned to Hope. "I meant you—alone—sweetheart. You could get another hour or two of sleep. The camera crews won't be here until the afternoon."

Her slender shoulders squared in fierce defiance. "No. I need to shower and get into work clothes, so as soon as Max goes to sleep, I'll be doing that."

Okay, then. "How about I watch him for you while you do all that?"

Gratitude shone in her eyes. "There are times like now when I don't know how I'm ever going to repay you."

Resisting the urge to really kiss her, he offered a wicked

smile instead. "Not to worry," he whispered in her ear. "I'll collect."

This time she smiled back, just as mischievously. "I am sure you will."

HOPE CLIMBED INTO the shower and let the hot water pour over her. She knew she had been moody lately—that Garrett had attributed it to lack of sleep and hormones, when, in fact, what she was worried and sad about was the fact that the job with the Lockharts was coming to a close. She and Max would be leaving, and she might never see Garrett again. Or she would see him, from time to time, but it wouldn't be the same. Hadn't she promised herself she wasn't going to do this again? Launch herself into a love affair that was only destined to end?

She had told Garrett—and herself—she could handle it. That this fling was all she wanted. Or needed. Now she was beginning to see it wasn't true. She did want to get married. She wanted a husband to share the good and bad times with. She wanted Max to have a daddy. And she wanted that daddy to be…Garrett?

Not because he was so good with Max.

Or because he seemed to genuinely like having kids around.

But because Garrett just fit into their lives. And their hearts.

Worse, her body tingled with need for him every time she was near him. It had been thirty hours since they had last made love, yet it felt like forever. Of course that was probably just her hormones. It had to be, Hope told herself, as she toweled off and dressed for work, then went out to the main living area of the bunkhouse. Max was on the counter in his infant seat, watching Garrett and Sage alternately cook breakfast together and jockey for space.

"I keep telling Max that the kitchen is mine," Sage joked, looking every bit as enthralled with Hope's son as her brothers and mother. "And Garrett should just go put his feet up somewhere."

"Hey," Garrett claimed, with an elbow to his sister's side, "I'm quite the chef in my own right."

Hope found herself leaping in to defend him. "He really is."

Sage scoffed. "You say that now, but you haven't tasted my food yet."

Lucille walked out, still looking wrung out and exhausted, despite over twelve hours of sleep. "It's true." The older woman flashed a wan smile. "Although both Sage and Garrett are excellent chefs."

Curious, Hope asked, "Did you teach them?"

Lucille, who—like Hope—had already dressed for the interview to come at noon that day, adjusted her pearls. "Oh, no, I can't cook at all."

"Gladys, our cook, taught us when Mom and Dad were out evenings," Sage explained.

Lucille reached for the coffee pot. Her hand was trembling slightly. "There was a serious lack of family dinners when our children were growing up."

Garrett had said as much. Hope found that sad. So did the Lockhart matriarch.

Sage and Garrett hugged Lucille simultaneously. Garrett soothed, "Not to worry, Mom. We're making up for it now."

Lucille's smile faltered.

"Lucille?" Hope asked, not sure what the sudden pale shift in the sixty-eight-year-old woman's color meant. "Are you feeling okay?"

Lucille gasped. "I...don't know..." She put her hand to her chest, winced, as if in horrendous pain.

"Oh, my God, Mom!" Sage rushed toward her mother.

Lucille staggered slightly. "I think I'm having a heart attack!" she said.

Garrett caught his mother as she fell.

"EXHAUSTION. DEHYDRATION. HYPERVENTILATION. All of which led to one heck of an episode of tachycardia," Laramie Community Hospital emergency room doctor Gavin Monroe pronounced, after examining Lucille. Her children gathered round.

"So it wasn't a heart attack?" Hope blurted out before she could stop herself.

She knew she wasn't family, but at this moment she felt like it.

"No. It just mimicked one," Dr. Monroe explained. "Given what Mrs. Lockhart has been through the last few weeks, it's not surprising she is at her limit."

"What's the treatment plan?" Garrett asked, still cradling Max in his arms.

Dr. Monroe said, "Sleep is the most important thing. We're giving your mother a sedative and admitting her for at least twenty-four…maybe forty-eight hours, depending on how she does. That will help enormously. So will getting her out of the previous stressful environment. Try to see that she follows a healthy diet and has lots of family support. Exercise. We'll also have her evaluated to make sure she's not suffering from anxiety or depression. If she is, those can both be treated medically."

A mixture of guilt and worry filled Hope. This was partly her fault for not being able to take enough of the burden off the shoulders of the Lockhart matriarch. And not listening to Garrett when he tried to convince her and his mother to get more sleep. She couldn't do anything about that now, but she could take extra strides to protect her from this point forward. "Should Lucille be admitted under a fictitious name?"

Brows lifted, all around.

Hope staved off interruption with a lift of her hand. "I know there are medical privacy laws to protect patients."

Sternly, Dr. Monroe said, "And we take them very seriously."

"I'm sure you do," Hope countered, "but Mrs. Lockhart has been in the news a lot lately, and not in a positive way. When there is an ongoing crisis of this nature, things like a 'nervous collapse' or 'sudden hospitalization' have a way of leaking to the press."

Gavin Monroe gave Hope a censoring look. "In Laramie, Texas, we take care of our own. And anyone who happens to be just passing through, as well. But," he continued kindly, "if you-all like, I'll speak to the staff. See that Mrs. Lockhart is listed in the hospital visitor register under her maiden name, Henderson."

"We'd appreciate that," Garrett said.

Dr. Monroe nodded. "In the meantime, you all need to go home and let Lucille get some much-needed rest."

Reluctantly, they all returned to the ranch.

They'd barely gotten out of their vehicles when two news vans with satellite hookups attached to the roofs caravanned down the drive.

Sage gasped. "Oh, no. I almost forgot!"

Hope hadn't.

Sage swung around. "What are we going to tell the reporter about Mom?"

Garrett looked at Hope. "Why don't we let Hope tell us?" he suggested quietly.

Chapter Thirteen

It meant a lot to Hope, that Garrett—and his siblings—trusted her to protect their mother to the best of her ability.

"The goal here is to preserve Lucille's privacy. Keep what should be confidential out of the public domain."

Garrett kept his eyes locked with hers. "You're asking us to parse the truth?"

Hope did her best to contain the protective emotion welling up inside her. She'd come to care for Lucille, too. "I'm asking you to reveal only what you think would be okay with your mom. Right now, if we were to let the press know she had been hospitalized for exhaustion—"

"They'd be camped outside the county medical center. Trying to get shots of us coming in and out," Chance predicted grimly.

"Right," Wyatt chimed in. He placed an arm around his younger sister's shoulders. "And none of us want that."

Hope searched Garrett's face. Although his expression remained implacable, she could only imagine the conflict this was causing him, deep inside. "Look, I know you agreed to take the lead here, as the eldest son and the male head of the family, but if you're not comfortable with this, I can prepare a statement. We can cancel the interview and go with that."

He regarded her for a long, thoughtful moment. "Won't

that stir up more interest, instead of less, since we've already agreed to do the interview?"

Hope sighed. "Probably."

"Then we really need to follow through as promised," he decided.

"Besides," Sage told Garrett, "you are a doctor. You're used to protecting a patient's privacy. This is no different than that, really."

It shouldn't have been, Hope thought. But she could tell he was uncomfortable with the whole idea of trying to hide things from the press. Nevertheless, he was first in line to meet the TV reporter, Nikki Lowell, who'd had the camera crew filming from the moment she stepped out of the news van.

Looking as handsome as ever, Garrett strode forward to shake Nikki's hand. Grinning widely, his sea-blue eyes crinkling at the corners, he turned on the full Lockhart charm.

Enough to make Hope feel a twinge of relief. She knew in that instant that Garrett was going to put his own personal feelings aside and step up to master the task at hand. Even if it wasn't anything he would have ever chosen to do.

Once all the introductions had been made, Nikki asked, "Where's Lucille?"

Garrett explained Lucille had been unavoidably detained, but sent her apologies. "The truth is, my mother is worn out from the events of the last week and a half. I'm sure you can understand how hectic a schedule she has kept, personally meeting with all the directors of the charities who were let down, making good on their long-delayed fiscal gifts."

"Why did she do that?" Nikki asked, signaling for the camera crew to zoom in on Garrett's handsome face. "I mean, she could have left it to anyone else, even the lawyers."

Not Lucille's style, Hope thought proudly.

"As CEO, she felt personally responsible," Garrett said.

"Do you think Lucille should have known what was going on a whole lot sooner?" Nikki asked.

"I don't deal in what-ifs," he said quietly.

Hope knew that to be all too true.

As much as she might wish otherwise, Garrett wasn't the kind of man who would spend time wishing that he and she had met and become involved under wildly different circumstances.

As far as he was concerned, their affair was what it was. Just as this confrontation with Nikki and the TV network news could not be avoided. They would battle their way through it, even if doing so meant uncomfortably parsing every word.

Nikki tilted her head, as if trying to figure out how to get under Garrett's skin and uncover what she suspected was being kept from her and the rest of the media. "Do you think your mom should have skipped out on the scheduled interview today, whether she felt up to being here or not?" Nikki asked.

Sage, Wyatt and Chance moved in close to the eldest Lockhart. United, they were an impressive front. Garrett folded his arms in front of him and stared down Nikki Lowell with a warrior's ease. "My siblings and I all agree our mother's health comes first." His brothers and sister nodded in support.

Nikki turned to Hope.

"When this family bands together there is no stopping them," Hope informed her. "I did discuss the possibility of rescheduling so we could have the interview conducted as originally planned, but they were anxious to let people know what's been discovered about the fraud."

"I can understand that," Nikki said.

Hope sighed in commiseration. "And with the Dallas

Police Department now actively beginning an investigation into the embezzlement, as of late last evening, it's only a matter of time before some other news outlet discovers the scoop we're giving you, so…"

Reminded that she and Hope had worked with each other on previous scandals, and Hope had always been as straightforward as possible with her, Nikki regarded Hope, one professional to another. "You're right. We can always add to the story later. Let's do it."

Everyone sat down in the Adirondack chairs in the backyard. With the breathtaking view of the ranch behind them, Nikki started with a few easy questions, then asked, "How was it possible to have twenty-five million dollars stolen without anyone noticing?"

"My parents wanted to avoid spending a lot of money on overhead for the foundation, so the Lockhart Foundation had very little staff." Garrett went on to explain how the CFO had handled all the financial activities. "My mother signed all the checks, but she trusted Paul Smythe—who was also an old family friend—to handle the rest."

"In other words, your parents' noble intentions and generosity made fraud possible."

All four Lockhart siblings nodded.

"What now?" Nikki continued. "Are you going to close the foundation?"

"No," Garrett said firmly. "Absolutely not."

"But if the bank accounts have been emptied…"

The siblings exchanged looks. It seemed, Hope noted happily, they were all of one opinion.

"We'll find a way to keep it going," Garrett promised.

THE REST OF the afternoon was spent showing Nikki and her film crew the Circle H ranch. When evening came, the news crew departed and the family enjoyed a brief dinner together, then Sage went to the hospital to check on her mother. Wyatt and Chance left for their own ranches to tend to their herds. Only Hope, Garrett and Max remained at the Circle H.

"Did you mean that—about finding a way to keep the foundation going, as a family?" Hope asked, after putting a sleeping Max to bed. "And not just leaving it to your mother?"

"Yes." Garrett continued loading the dishwasher.

Seeing the opportunity to finally check this off her To Do list, she went to lend a hand. "Because there is something your mother hoped I would be able to talk you into doing," she continued bluntly, knowing it was a risk to even try and broach this subject.

She waited until his steady blue gaze met hers.

"Becoming CEO in Lucille's stead."

He studied her in a weighted, awkward silence, looking anything but pleased. Then he scoffed and shook his head. "You really expect us to ask my mother to be the scapegoat in this mess and resign? After all she's been through? After how hard she's fought the last couple of weeks to make things right?"

Ignoring the temper in his tone, Hope worked to keep her cool. "She made the decision days ago." She paused, to let that sink in. "Lucille's reputation as a manager is tainted, most likely irreparably. She understands she can still be a member of the board and she can help out behind the scenes. But the reality is that unless someone like you—a doctor with a distinguished military background—takes over and becomes the public face of the foundation, gets everything back on track, the organization's chances of survival are not good. Particularly if, in order to continue, you-all are going to have to rely on fund-raising instead of family money."

Grimacing he picked up the recycling container and headed outside. "A couple of problems with that. I'm lousy at soliciting money."

She could see that. Garrett wasn't the kind of guy to go cap in hand to anyone.

She also noticed that he hadn't said he wasn't interested in the job at all.

She followed with a bag of regular trash. "You can hire professionals for that."

"With what?" Garrett dropped both in the appropriate containers. "There's no money left, remember?"

They turned and walked back toward the bunkhouse. The sun was setting in a streaky pink-and-purple sky. The summer air was fragrant with the smells of sunshine, flowers and freshly mown grass. "I'm assuming, like your siblings, that at least some eventually will be recovered. If not, where there's a will, there's a way. Charities do it all the time."

His look let her know there was an even bigger obstacle.

He dropped down onto the glider on the back porch, stretching his long legs out in front of him.

Hope left the back door slightly ajar so she'd be able to hear Max if he needed her.

Garrett massaged the back of his neck. "I don't want to work in Dallas."

Where Max and I live.

Another arrow to the heart.

Hope forced herself to be a professional and continued lobbying for her client. "So hire a staff you like, move wherever you like." *Even if it is thousands of miles from me and Max.* "Run the Lockhart Foundation from afar."

Garrett studied her. Finally he asked quietly, "Somewhere like Washington, DC?"

Hope wasn't sure whether the question was rhetorical—or a test. She did know she didn't want Lucille to lose out on a great solution to their problems because their scandal manager had bungled it by pushing too hard, or not enough.

"We did some checking," she told Garrett carefully, trying not to notice how handsome he looked in his pale blue button-down, jeans and boots. "You can work for any charity you like, while still on active duty in the military, as long as there is no conflict of interest with your service to our country, and we would have the lawyers make sure that there would not be. The same would be true if you were to take the hospital job in Seattle."

He shook his head. "I already turned that down."

Although she had known he was leaning that way, she hadn't realized he'd already made a final decision. Which made her wonder, what else hadn't he told her? Just how much *did* she know about him? And why was she suddenly so unnerved? They were involved in a fling, nothing more. So, at least from his point of view, it shouldn't really matter to her what his plans were, or vice versa.

Telling herself to cut both of them a break, Hope forced her thoughts back to the CEO position. "It wouldn't need to be a permanent situation, Garrett."

Just like their love affair, enthralling as it was, wasn't permanent.

"We just need a fresh face to go with a fresh start for the foundation. The board of directors can name you the interim CEO, to manage the implementation of new safeguards to prevent fraud in the future, and ease you out in a month or two, if you like."

His lips formed a more amenable line. "I can see where this would take a great deal of stress off my mother. Especially now, with her so exhausted." He turned to look at Hope. "But why didn't my mother broach this with me?"

A tricky point. Hope remained standing, her back to the wooden porch post, her hands behind her. "She was going to, eventually. But she thought the initial discussion might be better received coming from someone else."

Garrett waited, obviously sensing there was more.

With a reluctant sigh, Hope told him, "A pretty face."

He winced.

"Her words, not mine."

Garrett rolled to his feet. "You didn't mind being put in the middle of a family drama?"

Holding her ground, Hope shrugged. "Sometimes it's my job."

He ambled closer. "You're sure this is what my mother wants?"

He was so near, she had to tilt her head back to see into his face. "That, plus for all of her children to make good use of their inheritance from their father."

"I understand that for Chance and Wyatt. They're ranchers. Although she's the last person to admit it, Sage needs to be closer to her family. But for Zane—who's in the Special Forces—and me…? My mom really expects me to *reside* in Laramie?"

Was that even a possibility? Over a week ago he had been going to sell both his Laramie properties as soon as possible and move on.

Unable to clearly read his mood or expression, Hope moved away from the post and paced to the far end of the porch, where gorgeous flowers had been planted in advance of the film crew's arrival.

Drinking in the sweet, sun-drenched floral scent, Hope turned back to face him.

"If Laramie County is where you see yourself settling down, why not? You've already become involved in the community, in supporting one nonprofit organization here that you obviously feel passionately about—West Texas Warrior Assistance."

He downplayed his largesse. "I wrote a check."

It was more than that; she knew it, deep down. And so did he, if he would just admit it to himself.

Irritated that he wasn't telling her what was on his mind, she walked slowly toward him and said, "Chance showed me the specs on the office building you inherited on his phone yesterday afternoon, when you were in town clearing the trash out of the Victorian."

Another shrug of those powerful shoulders. Another poker face. "It's got to be fixed up to be leased out again."

Leased, not sold. Hope moved even closer and dared to push a little more. "We all figured out what you were doing."

Abruptly, Garrett became cynical and guarded, similar to the man she'd first met on the plane from DC. "Yeah?" he challenged dryly. "And what is that?"

"You're turning the office building into a place to house the WTWA."

When he didn't react, she pushed even more. "With what would appear to be an area for physical therapy and spaces on the upper floors for counseling and group therapy."

He remained where he was, legs braced apart, brawny arms folded in front of him. "So?"

"An undertaking that large is going to need a medical director to pull everything together. And my guess is you want it to be you."

GARRETT HAD NEVER met anyone who understood him the way Hope did. All week long he had been wondering if he was crazy, unrealistic, getting ahead of himself. Taking the guilt he felt over the way the foundation and his family had let Bess Monroe and the local former soldiers down by not fulfilling their promises, and turning it into what could be a life's mission for him.

He'd never been impulsive.

But here he was, after a little more than a week's time, taking his career objective and standing it on its head. And not just for the soldiers. No, there was a lot more driving this.

"It's true," he admitted carefully, letting his gaze rove over Hope. Because she'd been working in her official capacity as scandal manager all day—albeit in a rural environment—she was dressed in a black and sky-blue print cotton skirt that molded her hips and waist and ended just above the knee. A sleeveless white cotton blouse had been paired with a blue cardigan and flats. A heart-shaped gold necklace and earrings gleamed against the creamy alabaster of her skin. As the urge to make love to her again grew, his body tightened in response. How he wished he could simply take her to bed, instead of having this uncomfortable conversation.

But she wanted, needed to know where things stood with him, so…

He looked her in the eye. "Whether I'm active-duty military or not, I want to keep helping soldiers." *No matter what I'm doing, I can see myself still wanting you. And wanting to be a part of Max's life, too.*

"Which is why the job at Walter Reed held so much appeal to you, even if it meant reenlisting."

He walked close enough to inhale her sweet and sexy scent. "As much as I'd like to practice medicine there, I also know there will always be other doctors ready and willing to help out."

"You have good doctors and nurses here in Laramie County, too." They'd seen them in action—first caring for Max and then Lucille.

"What we don't have in Laramie County are programs designed exclusively for former military. In many ways, their needs are greater, because they are no longer in the armed services, yet many are still dealing with injuries and rehabilitation, and the process of making the transition back to civilian life."

Understanding lit her pretty emerald-green eyes. "You know you could make a difference."

He gently stroked her cheek with the back of his hand. "Which maybe is what my dad wanted all along when he left me the two properties."

She leaned into his touch. "For you to settle here?"

The silky warmth of her skin sent another wave of desire roaring through him.

He nodded. "And to help the people in Laramie County, where he and my mom grew up. He knew I had no ties to Dallas. That I'd never really fit there."

"But you do here."

Her compassion warmed him from the inside out. He let his hands slide to her shoulders. "Not sure I want to breed horses or bulls, like my brothers, but yeah… I like the Texas countryside a lot. And I like the house in town, too."

Smiling, she lifted her chin. "It's close to the hospital. And the office building."

It would be a good place to settle down one day and bring up a family, he thought, his gaze roving the softness of her lips. But wary of getting ahead of himself, scaring off Hope, who thus far had only agreed to a temporary liaison with him, he reined in his innate need to just say whatever was on his mind, and kept silent about that. For now. Garrett decided to show her what he felt, instead.

Chapter Fourteen

Garrett took Hope in his arms and kissed her until her abdomen felt liquid and weightless and her knees grew weak. He brought her against him, length to length. His tongue swept her mouth until her whole body was quivering with urgent need, her heart thumping so hard she could feel it in her ears.

And still he pressed her against him intimately, hardness to softness, until the last of her reservations regarding the wisdom of a short-term affair faded. She knew her task here would be over soon. But that didn't mean they couldn't make the most of what little time they had left.

Still kissing her ardently, he undid the buttons on her blouse, unfastened the front closure of her bra. He bent to kiss her chin, the arch of her neck, the uppermost curves of her taut, tingling breasts.

Around them, the sky grew dusky. The silence of the countryside as well as the warm, flower-scented air and faint summery breeze, provided a sensual setting.

It would be completely dark soon.

She didn't care. She wanted him.

Here. Now. Like this.

Spinning him around with a boldness she had not known she possessed, she pushed him beneath the overhang, up against the side of the house. Her eyes locked with his and she began unbuttoning his shirt.

He threaded his hands through her hair, watching. "And just when I thought you couldn't surprise me," he murmured.

She rose on tiptoe and, parting the edges of his shirt, pressed her bare breasts against the muscles of his chest. Wreathing her arms around his neck, she smiled wickedly. "Oh, I'm full of surprises."

Why not, since this was likely their last hurrah?

"Like this…" She fit her lips to his, opening her mouth, caressing his tongue, savoring the hot, masculine taste of him. Finding solace…finding strength…in tenderness.

Aware she had never felt as soft and womanly and empowered as she did with him, she unclasped his belt buckle and undid the zipper on his jeans. He moaned as she cupped the hard, velvety length of him in her palm. Stroking. Reveling. Enciting.

The next thing she knew, the back zipper of her skirt was coming undone, too. The floral fabric was sliding down over her knees. Pooling at her feet. A swift hook of his thumbs in the elastic and her panties followed.

"Hey. I'm supposed to be in charge here," she reminded him breathlessly.

He grinned and lifted both hands in ready and willing surrender. "Then I guess I'll have to let you have your way with me."

Deciding the only way to keep him where she wanted him was to trap him with her weight, she took his hand and directed him toward the glider.

A quick tug sent his jeans down his thighs. Leaving them at mid-knee, thus trapping him right where and how she wanted him, she settled on his lap, her arms encircling his shoulders, her thighs planted tight on either side of his.

"Now, where were we?" she murmured, kissing him again.

"Here?" The tip of his manhood pressed against her. "Or here?" Seconds later, his calloused palms moved slowly, lovingly upward over her ribs. "Or maybe here…?" Her nipples tingled as he bent and kissed her breasts. She moaned again, yearning to have him inside her.

This was torture.

Sweet torture.

But torture nevertheless.

"Maybe I will let you call the shots," she said, kissing him again, deeply, provocatively. "As long as it's—" she shifted wantonly to show him what she meant "—right now."

He grinned, his lips nipping at hers even as one hand slid between them. He refused to let her rush. "Not yet."

Gripping her buttocks with one hand, he spread her thighs all the more, stroked her inner thighs, made his way through the nest of soft curls to the softer petals hidden within. She shuddered, gasped as he sent her libido into overdrive.

And still he kissed her with maddeningly slow intensity until her blood flowed through her veins like liquid fire and her body pulsed and shuddered with exploding need.

With a groan, he brought her down over top of him. Pushed up into her, hard. Seeming to know, as always, exactly what she wanted and needed, he lifted her against him, thrust deep, let her settle, thrust deep again. Faster, then slower. Then perfect, so perfect. Her soul soaring as high as her heart, he possessed her on his terms. Refusing to let her run away, set unnecessary limits, he brought her to life. Again and again. Until at last his control faltered, too. They surged together, finding a pleasure so deep and profound it seemed impossible. And Hope knew that maybe—just maybe—she'd been wrong. This wasn't a short-term love affair, after all.

It was one that would last.

All she had to do was open up and take a risk.

With her heart. With her life…

And maybe Garrett would, too.

MORNING BROUGHT WITH it a flurry of activity. While Hope cared for Max and responded to journalists inquiring about the theft at the Lockhart Foundation, Garrett went into town to meet with Bess Monroe and the other founders of West Texas Warrior Assistance.

At noon, he returned to the ranch with his siblings and recovering mother in tow.

Not that Lucille had apparently accepted her physician's advice to take it easy. A fact that appeared to be irking her own doctor son to no end.

Garrett squared off with Lucille as she called everyone to the long plank table. "Mom, you just got home from the hospital. Now is not the time for a Lockhart Foundation board meeting."

Hope backed Garrett up. "I agree."

Although Lucille had slept nearly nineteen hours straight in the hospital before being released, the older woman still looked exhausted in a way that would take weeks to recover from. But, for the moment, as Lucille waved off her eldest son's concern, she was as fiercely determined as ever. "Nonsense! There are things we need to talk about—and vote on. I won't be able to rest until we do. And since my doctor's orders were "rest, rest, and more rest…""

With a groan, everyone sat down.

Hope started to exit the room.

Lucille waved her back. "No, Hope, you need to stay." Reluctantly Hope returned. "The first order of business is that I want you to be the new director of public relations at the Lockhart Foundation. A move that takes board approval."

Taken aback, Hope looked at the shocked faces all around her. "We probably should have talked about this beforehand. And you should have spoken with the board, too."

Had Hope not fallen hard for Garrett, she would have jumped at the opportunity. The fact that she was intimately involved with him made it all far too complicated.

Lucille scoffed. "And give you a chance to refuse me? No way. You need a job with more flexible hours. Recovering from the scandal is going to continue to be an uphill climb and we require your expertise."

Hope slipped into the open chair next to Sage and looked across the table at Garrett. He was so still he could have been playing a game of statue.

That did not seem like a good thing.

She battled a self-conscious blush and swallowed around the rising ache in her throat. Suddenly, she had to know. "Did you instigate this?"

He let out a long breath, shook his head.

Disappointment roiled through her. Why, she didn't know. Since when did she want anyone propelling her into a job that would likely upend her life more than it already had been the past few weeks?

She had Max to consider.

Well, that and her heart, which suddenly seemed to be in jeopardy, too.

Garrett rubbed his hand across his jaw, as if it were taking everything he had to contain himself. Dropping his hand, he met the gazes of everyone at the table. "Hope's right," Garrett said in a low, clipped tone. "We probably should have spoken about this. Since finding the funds for her salary could be a problem, given the current state of foundation bank accounts."

"I have a solution for that, too," Lucille announced with a brisk smile. "I'm selling my home in Dallas. Half the proceeds will go into a trust to fix up the Circle H, where I now plan to reside full time. That, plus the money from my retirement account will see me comfortably into old age. The other half will go to the foundation."

She paused for effect as she glanced around the room. "But this time, I don't want to try and work with one hundred charities. I just want to work with one. West Texas Warrior Assistance. If Garrett is going to be the medical director, we need to support him."

No problem there, Hope noted. Garrett's siblings were completely behind the idea.

"Let's vote on it," Sage enthused. "All in favor of hiring Hope, say aye."

A chorus of "Ayes!" came from around the table.

"And focusing the foundation on West Texas Warrior Assistance?"

Once again, the support was unanimous.

Sage made a note in the meeting minutes.

Hope cleared her throat. When she had everyone's attention, she asked, "Shouldn't you ask me if I want the job?"

"Ah, not just yet." Sage turned back to her mother. "Obviously, Mom, you've given this a lot of thought."

Lucille smiled. "I have. And for the record, I also want to install Adelaide, since she was instrumental in helping us uncover the fraud, as our new chief financial officer."

Wyatt frowned the way he always did when his former girlfriend's name came up. "We definitely need to talk about that."

Lucille leveled a look right back at Wyatt. "Oh, we will," she promised.

Garrett shook his head as if that would clear it. "Mom, what's gotten into you? You used to be so…restrained!"

"The last few weeks made me think about all the problems I couldn't solve, as well as the ones that we could, if we had just not swept problems under the rug and instead confronted them directly. And that brings me to my next agenda item." Lucille referred to her tablet. "Garrett, you've said you're willing to be CEO. Can you start immediately?"

He nodded, obviously willing to do whatever it took to allow his mother to concentrate on regaining her good health.

Lucille smiled her approval. "Everyone want to vote on the last two items?"

And with a quick vote the family gave its approval.

"Great." Lucille grinned at the four children gathered around her. "Now, what are we going to do about having Garrett, the new CEO, in Laramie, and Hope in Dallas? Hope, are you—and Max—willing to relocate? As soon as it's convenient, of course."

The matriarch of the family was definitely a steamroller. And she had just run roughshod over Hope. With all good intentions, certainly, but Hope still felt shell-shocked and uncertain.

Knowing she had to get her life problems figured out and solved on her own, Hope ignored the intentions and focused on the assessing way Garrett was looking at her. She lifted her chin. "Lucille, I appreciate your confidence in me, but I haven't even said I'd take the job yet."

"If we meet all your demands—salary, living arrangements, work hours, responsibilities and so forth—would you?"

Hope looked at Garrett, still having no clue as to how

he felt about all this. And that was the sticking point—not where she lived, or how much she made, or even how many job responsibilities she would have. She wanted to know what he felt. That he wanted to work side by side with her. Because if that wasn't the case…and the maddeningly inscrutable look on his face said maybe it wasn't…then any further discussion was pointless.

She'd grown up feeling in the way. She wasn't going to do it again.

"I don't know what I'd do. All I know is that I can't give you an answer today, not like this."

For a second, disappointment reigned.

Hope realized she hadn't been the only one secretly wishing she could be a permanent part of all this…

Sage looked at Garrett with a mixture of starry-eyed envy and approval. "Maybe it would help if you came clean." She prodded her eldest brother in the unabashedly romantic direction she wanted him to go. "Told everyone the two of you are…um…"

Lucille put in hopefully, "Serious about each other…? Engaged?"

It was all Hope could do not to groan. If Garrett's mother only knew how far from any kind of commitment, never mind any lasting future, she and Garrett were…

Lucille would be so disappointed.

As disappointed as Hope suddenly felt.

What happened in the darkness of his bedroom was one thing, to have it scrutinized in the glaring light of day, with the people who meant most to him gathered around, was another.

Garrett looked at Hope as if trying to read her mind. This time, she gave him nothing of what she was feeling, putting him on the hot seat, too, right along with her.

"No," he said finally. "It's too soon for that."

Lucille harrumphed, her disapproval as sharp as the glare she gave her son. "But not too soon to sleep with each other."

A collective gasp was followed by a beat of silence.

Ignoring Garrett's dark scowl, Lucille turned and focused on the blush blooming in Hope's cheeks. "I know two well-loved people when I see them."

Funny, Hope thought. Until now, she'd felt that way. She looked into his eyes and saw regret, and wondered if it was as painful as the remorse filling her heart. But there was no clue in the watchful silence of the room.

Garrett swung back to the members of the board, squared his shoulders and tried again. "I get that you're trying to help, Mom, but what Hope and I have shared is *not* up for family discussion. Nor is any aspect of her life or mine. I thought I had made that abundantly clear."

Suddenly, Hope didn't want their relationship to be something that could not be acknowledged or talked about. Even, or especially, to his family. To her surprise, she wanted one heck of a lot more. And she wanted it right now. Because if he didn't feel what she did, if he didn't even come close, then Lucille's unspoken accusation was right. What were they doing?

And to think she'd been worried about a succession of nannies! This was so much worse for her baby boy than that! Max deserved stability, and it was up to her to give it to him. He could not be expected to love and depend on Garrett, only to have the only father he had ever known walk away without warning. She and Garrett both had career decisions that needed to be made.

She'd been thinking he would factor into hers. Just as she had hoped she was factoring into his.

Had she been wrong? About that, how he felt, how he might ever feel?

Hope pushed back her chair and stood. Hands on the table in front of her, chin high, she asked, "Then how would you define it, if we're not engaged—" and apparently not headed that way, judging by his continued stony reaction "—and not an item?"

Garrett shoved back his chair and moved effortlessly to his feet, too. They stared at each other across the wide plank table.

Aware the foundation board meeting had devolved into something else entirely, yet needing her questions answered, Hope put her usual decorum aside and pressed on without shame or discretion. "I mean if it's only a fling and you're okay with that…" And she wasn't, she realized far too late, not at all! "Shouldn't you be able to own up to that?" She gestured at their audience. "I mean we're all adults here. Right?"

An even tenser silence fell.

Lucille stared at her son, waited.

"Ah. Maybe we should call an end to the board meeting and leave." Sage scrambled to her feet.

"Or better yet, maybe we should get out the popcorn." With an ornery grin, Wyatt stayed put.

Chance rocked back in his seat, arms folded in front of him. "I'd like to hear this, too," Chance said. "Might learn something. About what not to do, obviously."

"It's *private*." Garrett pushed the words through clenched teeth.

Hope's heart pounded as if she'd run a marathon, even as her spirits sank. She held Garrett's gaze, ready to put it all on the line for the very first time in her life. If only he would dare to do so, too.

But that, she could tell, would only happen if she forced him.

Fighting through her disappointment, she pushed on

like a reporter in a hostile press conference, "*Private* as in doesn't exist?"

He gave her no reaction.

Fighting tears, Hope offered another choice. "Never happened? Never should have happened?"

Because ethically, morally, she knew the answer to that even if he hadn't hired her and couldn't fire her.

Oh, heavens above, what a mess they had made.

WHAT DID HOPE want from him? Garrett wondered, grinding his jaw in frustration. Without warning, he felt as if he'd been propelled back to his childhood. Filled with all those unspoken and implied expectations he couldn't figure out, never mind meet. When he'd unfortunately blurted out whatever came to mind and gotten himself in even more trouble. Every time.

Determined not to do this, and certainly not in front of his whole family, he stood there, silent, just waiting, just looking at Hope. Waiting for her to give him a clue as to what would fix this. Not just with his family, who were more confused than he was, but with the two of them.

Usually, she was pretty good about doing that.

Not today.

And after the way they'd made love the night before? All night long? What was going on with her, with them? How had he managed once again to end up so completely blindsided and confused?

Giving her one more chance to fully illuminate this matter before he hauled her off to continue this discussion in private, Garrett finally asked with forced calm, "What do you want this to be?"

Another sad silence fell.

Hope, looking more disillusioned and disappointed than

he ever could have imagined her, simply shook her head. She looked him right in the eye, long and hard, and said, "Not. This."

Chapter Fifteen

Two days later, Lucille Lockhart stood in the bathroom of the former rental home and gaped at her eldest son. She was recovering nicely from her bout of exhaustion, getting stronger and healthier every day.

Garrett felt his own life going in reverse.

"You were serious about cleaning the bathrooms yourself."

Garrett dropped his scrub brush into the bucket, stripped off his gloves and stepped back. The entire upstairs of the Victorian house reeked of hospital-grade disinfectant. But the hours he'd spent working out his aggression had left it sparkling clean from top to bottom.

Thanks to the help he had received at the local hardware store, he also knew a lot more about home maintenance than he ever had before.

Had Hope elected to stick around, that skill might have come in handy. Since she hadn't…

He gathered up the rest of his gear, headed downstairs. "Why would you think I wasn't serious?" *About becoming more family oriented? Learning skills that would help with that—in a very practical way? Settling down?*

"Maybe you had better things to do with your time?"

He slid his mother a glance. "Like what?"

"Speaking to Hope?"

If he'd thought it would do any good, he would have. "She made it pretty clear when she left the Circle H she had nothing more to say to me."

"And you're content to leave it at that?"

No, but it was what he had to do, needed to do, to come out of this relationship with even a shred of dignity. Hope had been honest with him from the first. Told him her life was too chaotic and full, as it was. That she had her son, who was all she needed. That even if she wanted to embark on a relationship with him, which she clearly hadn't, she wouldn't have the time or the energy to be able to do so.

He should have listened to her, instead of seducing her into what was to be a strictly physical relationship with a firm expiration date.

He had agreed with her stipulations because he had thought, deep down, that he would be able to change her mind. That, as time wore on and they got closer—and they *had* gotten closer—she would come to want the same things he did.

Only she hadn't.

And he had to live with his crushed expectations, hopes and dreams. Because it was his fault he hadn't listened to her at the outset.

Garrett crossed over to the cooler and pulled out a couple of icy-cold flavored waters. He wiped off the dampness with a paper towel and handed his mom one. "Hope and I had an agreement, Mom. What we had was going to be a short-term thing, and that was it."

Lucille took a small, dainty sip. "You don't think she changed her mind?"

He had a flash of the soft, sweet way Hope gazed up at him when they made love, and the fiercely determined way she had looked as she had left the Circle H to return to her life in Dallas. He knew his mother was invested in this, rightly or wrongly. She had tried to help them find a happy-ever-after, and even if her ploy hadn't worked she deserved credit for trying.

Garrett downed half the bottle in a single gulp. The hot persistent ache in his throat only grew. He shrugged. "She never said so if she did."

His mother edged closer. She studied him with an eagle eye, before asking the kind of question she would have been too refined to have voiced before. "Did you change yours?"

The ever-present heaviness inside his heart remained. What did it matter? "It takes two equally committed people to make a successful relationship, Mom. You and Dad taught me that." It was what he wanted, what he had to have.

Lucille gazed at him thoughtfully, looking glad that at least one of her life lessons had sunk in. "Hope turned down the job at the foundation. Not because it wasn't challenging enough or would require her to relocate to Laramie, Texas. She turned it down because of you, Garrett."

Was he that much of a pariah? Did she still feel he had treated her poorly? Garrett clenched his teeth. "She didn't want to work with me?"

"She said she couldn't bear to be that close to you."

He stared at his mother like a shell-shocked idiot. "Hope actually said that?"

His mother propped her hands on her hips. "While she was crying her eyes out."

He took a moment to consider that. It was both the saddest thing and the best thing he had ever heard. Finally he found his voice, demanded thickly, "Hope cried over me?"

Lucille scoffed, as if she couldn't believe how oblivious he was. "You broke her heart!"

The accusation stung. And more, was completely unfounded. What had he done, after all, but offer Hope everything of value he had to give? All within the parameters she had set. "She decimated mine!"

Lucille leaned closer. "So tell her."

If he hadn't already been turned inside out, he would have. But he had, so…

Forcing himself to be realistic in a way he hadn't been before, Garrett shook his head. A reconciliation wasn't in the script Hope had laid out for them. And she was a woman who always stuck to the plan, never more so than when times got stressful. It was the only way to survive and come out unscathed, she had said.

Garrett winced. "She'd never believe me."

His mother encouraged him kindly. "Then it's up to you to tell her what's really in your heart and change that, isn't it?"

ON SATURDAY, HOPE left Max at home with a sitter and walked into the Lockhart Foundation for the last time. Lucille had asked her to pack up her personal belongings in advance of the mover's arrival.

Hope had readily agreed. Not only was it a way to help the still physically rebounding former CEO, but a way to give herself desperately needed closure, too.

As promised, Sharla, Lucille's soon-to-be-ex assistant, greeted Hope at the door.

Like Hope, she was in casual clothing, suitable for packing and moving.

They chatted for a moment, about who was tasked with packing up what and how, and Sharla's need to leave shortly to pick up her daughter after her ballet class.

Sharla led Hope over to the unassembled book boxes, markers, tape and scissors. While the two worked to put some boxes together, Sharla chatted. "I saw the video you posted on all the social media websites. You did a great job giving the history of the foundation and really introducing the entire family. I especially liked the way you portrayed Garrett. Sometimes he comes off as grumpy rather than heroic, but you caught his true essence."

Maybe because I know who he is, deep down. One of the kindest, strongest, most gallant men on Earth.

"Thanks."

"I was surprised you didn't take the public relations job for the foundation. Things had been going so well, from the sound of it."

They had been, for a while, anyway, Hope thought. In fact, she easily could have imagined herself becoming an integral part of the family charity.

Sharla chatted casually. "Is it because, like me, you didn't want to move to West Texas?"

"I just wasn't sure it was a good fit." *With me crazy in love with Garrett, and him feeling, I don't know exactly what, about me...*

Hope held a box closed while Sharla taped it shut. "What about you? Lucille told me you have a fantastic new job."

Nodding, Sharla grinned. "I start Monday. I've got a bump up in salary and responsibility, and a much shorter commute. Lucille really pulled out all the stops to make sure I wouldn't spend any time unemployed."

"Sounds like her," Hope said fondly.

"I know. All the Lockharts have huge hearts."

Even more importantly, the Lockharts had shown her what it was like to have a loving, supportive family surrounding you. They'd made her realize what she wanted in her own life—a love that would last, a daddy for Max, a family like theirs. Moreover, they'd helped her see that, in insisting on forging on alone, she was settling for far less than what either she or Max deserved.

And that meant changes had to be made, Hope schooled

herself firmly. No more dead-end love affairs. No more falling for guys who weren't falling for her just as hard.

Aware Sharla was waiting for more of an explanation, about how Hope could be so close to the family one week, and then working so furiously to distance herself from them, Hope said in a low tone, "Crises can bond people together intensely in the moment. Those feelings rarely last."

How often had she said those very words? And found them true?

Sharla fit bubble-wrapped pictures of her family into a box. "You're not friends with any of the people you've helped in the past?"

Hope began taking plaques bearing Lucille's name off the wall. "Not the way we were when the scandal or situation was in progress, no."

"That's too bad," Sharla sympathized.

It was. She needed more concrete relationships in her life. More people she and Max could rely on through thick and thin. Otherwise, her son was likely to grow up feeling as alone as she had when she was a child.

"I thought you and Garrett were getting, well, close."

They had been, Hope thought ruefully. She'd actually started to put herself out there instead of sticking to the script. She'd made the cardinal sin of allowing the overwhelming emotion of the crisis itself to influence her actions, as they had Garrett's.

If they'd simply had a casual fling, and ended it when they'd agreed that they would, without complication or hurt feelings, maybe they could have remained friends. Maybe she would have been able to move to Laramie, and see and work with Garrett every day. Let Garrett be a constant, loving male role model in Max's life.

And that might have left open the possibility that maybe, over time, as life returned to normal, they would *both* realize they wanted to take a chance on each other, this time with no holds barred.

But that wasn't ever going to happen, Hope realized again with a pang as she said goodbye to Sharla and worked on alone.

When confronted by his family, Garrett had taken an immediate and decisive step back. A move that had, sadly, told her all she needed to know.

He'd decided to settle close to his family, after all, and make good use of his inheritance, just the way his late father had wanted him to do.

He'd found a way to open up his heart. Just not to her. Not the way she wanted.

And she knew now that she couldn't settle for half measures. Not when it came to Garrett. She wanted it all with him, or she wanted nothing at all. Twenty minutes later, Hope had taken the last of the awards off the wall when she heard the door to the suite open and close.

Thinking Sharla had forgotten something, Hope stepped out into the reception area. There stood Garrett. Handsome as ever, big as life. Like her, he was in jeans and sneakers, and a loose-fitting cotton shirt worn open at the throat.

He looked good, too.

Freshly shaven, his hair cut, blue eyes glinting with the masculine determination she found so appealing.

"This was a setup," she deduced, her heart squeezing hard.

He nodded. "Engineered by me." As he strolled toward her purposefully, his sexy grin widened. "I have to tell you, my mother did not want to help me."

Tears misted her eyes and joy rose inside her. Even though she knew it was too soon for that. Might not even be the right time.

She swallowed around the lump in her throat and did

her best to appear cavalier. Tilting her head, she looked him up and down, as if she found him wanting. "Obviously, you convinced her."

"Once she listened to all I had to say." He squinted. "The question is, will you?"

Fear moved past the excitement roaring through her. She knew she couldn't bear it if he disappointed her again. She regarded him steadily, her guard up. "I think we said all we had to say during the board meeting." That she never should have been invited to attend, because then she wouldn't have heard all the questions, or seen him hedge.

Wouldn't have had everyone bear witness to her humiliation and heartbreak.

He came closer still, his eyes level on hers. "Not quite," he said softly but firmly.

Her heart pounded all the harder.

His eyes were full of things she was almost afraid to read as he took her hands in his. "I've never had trouble saying what was on my mind." The tips of his fingers caressed the back of her hands, eliciting tingles. "You may have heard," he continued, his voice a low, sexy rumble, "I'm blunt to a fault."

Hope hitched in a breath, suddenly afraid of where this might be going. "Except for the last time we saw each other," she reminded him, surprised she could sound so brave when inside she was on the verge of falling apart. *Again.* She lifted her chin. "Then you had no words."

Regret flashed on his handsome face. He nodded ruefully, his gaze narrowing. "Part of that was because I didn't want my family interfering in my life, or yours, and trying to engineer either of us into doing what *they* felt we should be doing."

Hope understood that.

The Lockhart clan had put them on the spot. Well-intentioned or not, the move had been a complete disaster.

Knowing he still had his own reticence to account for, she swallowed. "And the rest?"

"I was trying to follow your lead. Be sensitive. Discreet in a way I've never been before. Now, I'm here to lay my soul bare and tell you exactly what's on my mind," he said, his voice firm and strong. "First, I realize that holding back on what we are both thinking and feeling is never going to be right. Not for me, not for you, not for us."

She fought back a grin as her heart kicked against her ribs.

He wrapped both his arms around her waist. "I can still be tactful," he said, drawing her close, "but you need to tell me what's on your mind and in your heart, and I need to do the same." His voice dropped to a husky timbre. "So we're not caught off guard. Or left guessing what the other person is thinking or feeling."

"Agreed."

"So here's what's on my mind. No more scripts for either of us to follow. We both have to agree to wing it in the most genuine of ways to avoid miscommunication."

"You have given this a lot of thought!"

He waggled his brows as if to say *Just wait!*

"Next, as far as business goes, I want you to come to Laramie and work with me on both the WTWA and the relaunch of the much smaller but entirely laudable Lockhart Foundation. It will require you wearing two hats, being public relations director for both, but the hours will be entirely flexible to accommodate Max, and the offices are all going to be in the professional building I own, when the repairs are finished, which are apt to take about three months."

She splayed her hands across his chest. Felt his heart beating as hard as her own. "And until then…?"

"The WTWA will be working out of the Victorian. Renovations will be going on there, too, mostly on the weekends, but Max can come to work with you as much as you want, and there will be a place for you and Max at the Circle H bunkhouse, where you can live rent free."

It was nearly perfect. And yet…she knew she still had to have—they had to have—more.

But if that meant giving a little, too. Slowing down. Waiting to see what developed…

She could do that.

Yes, she could.

Because some things—some people—were worth waiting for.

"As family friends…?" Hope asked.

Because she and Max definitely fell into that category.

"No, sweetheart." Garrett shook his head. "As the woman I was meant to spend the rest of my life with." Raw emotion glimmered in his eyes. He wove his fingers through her hair and tilted her face up to his. "I love you, Hope," he told her hoarsely. "I have since the first moment you landed in my lap."

He pulled her up and into him. She rose even higher and met his lips in a searing kiss. Wrapping her arms around him, she tucked her face into the crook of his neck, shivering at the delight she felt being with him again.

"I love you, too," she whispered, drinking him in. His heat, his size, the brisk, masculine scent of him. She released a shuddering breath, savoring the feel of his hands moving over her. "I should have told you earlier."

He stroked a hand down her spine. His voice as tender as his touch, he asked, "Why didn't you?"

Hope drew back. Her arms resting on his broad shoulders, she looked deep into his eyes. It was time to let the defenses go. To dare the way he had. "It was all just so complicated." She shook her head with remembered misery. "I wasn't sure if what we had discovered was strong enough to last past the crisis."

A wry smile started on his lips and lit his eyes. "It is." He bent his head and kissed the top of her head, her temple. His thumbs caressed the line of her chin. "It definitely is."

He was so confident. She forced herself to admit with wrenching honesty, "Most of all, I was afraid to put myself out there all the way. Afraid of what would happen to us if I put it all on the line and you didn't love me back." Tears misted her eyes. "I didn't want to lose you."

His eyes crinkled at the corners, and he gave her a confident smile that she felt in every iota of her being. "You won't." He lifted his brow mischievously. "And to that end…" He reached into his pocket and drew out a velvet jewelry box, pressed it into her shaking fingers.

Inside was a beautiful diamond ring.

The sparkle of the gem was nothing compared to the brightness in his gaze. "Say you'll marry me, Hope," he rasped.

Was there any question? She grinned, a grin big as all Texas. "I will."

They shared another kiss. Long, lingering, sweet.

He cupped her face in his big, gentle hands, rested his forehead on hers. "So, it's agreed. From now on—" he kissed her cheek, nose, ear, with the kind of slow deliberation that always preceded the most mind-blowing lovemaking "—to avoid future misunderstandings, we both promise to always speak our minds. And encourage each other to do the same."

Not following a preordained script suddenly felt very,

very good. Her heart melted a little more. How had he gotten so wise? "I think I can handle that."

"Good." He tipped her face up to his and looked into her eyes until her knees went weak and joy bloomed within her. "Because I can't imagine a life without you and Max."

Hope kissed him back, promising, "You'll never have to…"

Epilogue

Six months later...

"Come on, buckaroo," Garrett crooned from the opposite side of the third-floor party room in the office building that now held both the Laramie Foundation offices and West Texas Warrior Assistance. Hunkered down affably, both hands outstretched toward their son, he encouraged cheerfully, "Walk to Daddy."

Eager to share what she had seen just a few hours earlier, Hope helped her wildly grinning nine-month-old son balance on the soles of his feet. "Show him what a talented boy you are." When Max seemed completely steady, she slowly and carefully released his hands.

Max let out a joyous whoop, swayed slightly and then shifted backward, landing squarely on his diapered bottom, as if that were the plan all along. He clapped his hands. And whooped again, Texas cowboy style.

His spirit was infectious. Hope and Garrett clapped and yee-hawed, too.

Max shifted quickly to his knees and crawled rapidly over to his daddy's side. Garrett scooped him up in his arms. "Good job, little fella!"

Max threw back his head and chuckled again.

Hope joined in the family hug. Briefly, she leaned her head on Garrett's chest. "I swear. Max was doing it earlier."

Garrett put a squirming Max back down so he could explore again. Immediately, Max crawled to a window ledge and pulled himself up to a standing position. "I believe you."

Hope put her hands on her hips, while Max thought about walking sideways using the wall for balance, as he had been doing for a good two months now. Then he changed his mind, sat down, flipped and began crawling again.

This was ridiculous.

Hope shook her head, laughing. She met the indulgent arch of Garrett's brow. "No. You don't."

And probably with good reason. She was always jumping the gun and seeing progress that wasn't quite there yet.

Sage breezed in with a tray of goodies for their first annual Day Before Thanksgiving party. "Have you met this man?" She peeled back the plastic wrap and offered Garrett a taste. He gave the cranberry, pecan and cream cheese appetizer quiches a thumbs-up. Hope nodded her approval, too. Grinning, Sage put the tray aside. "All he does is brag about you and Max."

Darcy and Tank walked into the group meeting room. The usual circle of chairs had been pushed back to the walls to allow for maximum dining space. Winking, Darcy spread tablecloths over the double row of buffet tables in the center of the room. "I think Hope might have had a few kind words to say about her hubby, too."

With good reason, Hope thought. No longer afraid to say what was on her mind, she swept her son up in her arms and walked over to buss Garrett's jaw. "Sage's big brother is a wonderful husband."

Wyatt and Chance appeared in the doorway. A chorus of male groans sounded. "Tell me they're not getting mushy again," Wyatt complained, strolling in.

"Yeah, you-all have been married for three months now. Enough already!" Chance said with a mischievous wink. "The honeymoon is over."

"It'll never be over," Garrett vowed.

Everyone groaned again—in humorous approval.

Lucille walked in, a horn of plenty in one hand, a big basket of fruit in the other.

She set both down on a buffet table and turned to her beloved grandson. "Want to show your nana how you can walk?" she said.

"Not quite there yet," Garrett told her.

"Maybe it was an anomaly," Hope reluctantly admitted.

Max pulled himself up on Garrett's legs, turned around, balanced briefly on the balls of his feet and took off for his grandmother. One step, two. Everyone held their breaths. Then he swiveled and headed right back to Garrett and Hope.

Tears of joy pouring down their faces, they watched him toddle all the way to their sides. One arm wrapped around each of their knees, he chortled and looked up at them.

Everyone cheered.

Max pulled on their legs, his signal he wanted to be picked up. Garrett lifted their son in his arms. Hope kissed his cheek.

Puzzled, Max tracked the happy tears pouring down both their faces while smiles flashed all around. Then he tucked a fist in the shirts of each of his parents. "Mine," he said fiercely.

"You bet we are," Garrett said fiercely.

"No question," Hope murmured, going in for a joyous group hug. "We have so much to be thankful for!"

* * * * *

Watch for the next story in Cathy Gillen Thacker's
TEXAS LEGACIES: THE LOCKHARTS *series,*
A TEXAS COWBOY'S CHRISTMAS, coming
soon from Mills & Boon Cherish!

MILLS & BOON®

Cherish™

EXPERIENCE THE ULTIMATE RUSH OF FALLING IN LOVE

A sneak peek at next month's titles...

In stores from 14th July 2016:

- **An Unlikely Bride for the Billionaire** – Michelle Douglas
  and **Her Maverick M.D.** – Teresa Southwick
- **Falling for the Secret Millionaire** – Kate Hardy *and*
  An Unlikely Daddy – Rachel Lee

In stores from 28th July 2016:

- **Always the Best Man** – Michelle Major *and*
  The Best Man's Guarded Heart – Katrina Cudmore
- **His Badge, Her Baby...Their Family?** – Stella Bagwell
  and **The Forbidden Prince** – Alison Roberts

Available at WHSmith, Tesco, Asda, Eason, Amazon and Apple

Just can't wait?
Buy our books online a month before they hit the shops!
visit www.millsandboon.co.uk

These books are also available in eBook format!

716/23

MILLS & BOON®

The One Summer Collection!

2 free books!

Join these heroines on a relaxing
holiday escape, where a summer fling
could turn in to so much more!

Order yours at **www.millsandboon.co.uk/onesummer**

0616_MB523_OSA

MILLS & BOON®

Mills & Boon have been at the heart of romance since 1908... and while the fashions may have changed, one thing remains the same: from pulse-pounding passion to the gentlest caress, we're always known how to bring romance alive.

Now, we're delighted to present you with these irresistible illustrations, inspired by the vintage glamour of our covers. So indulge your wildest dreams and unleash your imagination as we present the most iconic Mills & Boon moments of the last century.

Visit **www.millsandboon.co.uk/ArtofRomance** to order yours!

MILLS & BOON®

Why not subscribe?

Never miss a title and save money too!

Here is what's available to you if you join the exclusive **Mills & Boon® Book Club** today:

* *Titles up to a month ahead of the shops*
* *Amazing discounts*
* *Free P&P*
* *Earn Bonus Book points that can be redeemed against other titles and gifts*
* *Choose from monthly or pre-paid plans*

Still want more?

Well, if you join today we'll even give you
50% OFF your first parcel!

So visit **www.millsandboon.co.uk/subscriptions**
or call **Customer Relations on 0844 844 1351***
to be a part of this exclusive Book Club!

*This call will cost you 7 pence per minute plus your
phone company's price per minute access charge.

Lynne Graham has sold 35 million books!

To settle a debt, she'll have to become his mistress...

Nikolai Drakos is determined to have his revenge against the man who destroyed his sister. So stealing his enemy's intended fiancé seems like the perfect solution! Until Nikolai discovers that woman is Ella Davies...

Visit **www.millsandboon.co.uk/lynnegraham** to order yours!

MILLS & BOON®